POLISHING THE DIAMOND

Never Ride for Second

Jasper L Creakbaum

Copyright © *Jasper L Creakbaum,* 2024

All Rights Reserved

This book is subject to the condition that no part of this book is to be reproduced, transmitted in any form or means; electronic or mechanical, stored in a retrieval system, photocopied, recorded, scanned, or otherwise. Any of these actions require the proper written permission of the author.

Dedication

This project would not have been possible without two equally important facets. First, Diamond Amus (Amos) the most incredibly talented and beautiful Arabian horse that claimed me as his human counterpart early in his life. His desire to please, along with his skill in executing his abilities, made us a star in the show ring. Secondly, my wife, without her unselfish act of love brought Amos back for me because I so loved him. Along with her hard work, dedication to perfect execution of the discipline as well as trust in my encouragement in what Amos was capable of.

Author's Note

Father of two sons and three stepsons, eleven grandchildren, and three great-grandchildren, with two more on the way at the time of publishing of this book. I grew up on a small farm in the Midwest, where, at a young age, I became a total horse fanatic. I was involved in horses, riding and competing with them for most of my life. My love for horses guided me into the horse industry to make my living, first in training Tennessee Walking Horses and exhibiting at the highest levels. I later took my experience in horses and training to become a farrier. We currently reside in Alaska and enjoy our senior years catching fish and enjoying the beauty the State has to offer. We plan on moving to the Lower 48 to begin making memories with the great-grandchildren.

Table of Contents

Chapter 1: Laying The Groundwork 1

Chapter 2: Wheels Are Set In Motion 12

Chapter 3: School Begins 18

Chapter 4: School Of Higher Education 21

Chapter 5: Ready Or Not Here We Come! 31

Chapter 6: Time To Light This Candle 39

Chapter 7: A Storm Is Brewing 48

Chapter 8: Redemption At Last 52

Chapter 9: The Horse World Through The Eyes Of Michelle .. 59

Chapter 10: Ready Or Not: Here We Come Again! 72

Chapter 11: Into The Sunset 84

Chapter 12: Return To The Show Ring 95

Chapter 13: Git Along Little Dogie 108

Chapter 14: A Diamond Never Loses Its Shine 116

Chapter 1
Laying the Groundwork

Every story must have a beginning, so I would say this story started when I was 8 or 9 years old, growing up on a small family farm in northern Indiana. Looking back, I see my life as usual, growing up as a country kid. The family farm was not large but had an abundance of chores required by the dairy cattle, the hogs we raised, and the flock of sheep. I watched cartoons, rode bicycles with the neighbor kids, and was your typical neighborhood brat. One of my joys as a child was watching The Roy Rogers Show. I must admit Roy was my hero. Roy was always righting the wrongs of society, standing tall, being honest, and holding folks accountable; the lousy guy never won. Above all, Roy would never have accomplished these deeds without the assistance of Trigger, the Wonder Horse. I did not realize at that time how much Roy Rogers would affect my life from then on. My parents would ask me what I wanted for Christmas, and I answered, "A horse, of course."

When my birthday came around, my parents would ask me what I wanted for my birthday, and my answer was, "A horse, of course."

We did not own a horse, but I was fortunate enough to have an uncle with ponies that he had raised and trained to drive as a 4-hitch team. He would pull wagons, sleighs, and a stagecoach in parades, which was always delightful. But best of all, the ponies could be ridden, which was my ultimate pleasure. That was where my Roy Rogers persona began to shine.

Eventually, my parents caved to my relentless requests for a horse, which was nothing more than a small pony. He may have been a small pony, but in my eyes, he was just as big as Trigger and just as wonderful.

My parents had arranged for the delivery of the pony while I was at school. Once the bus had dropped me off at home, Mom told me to hurry up and change my clothes, as Dad needed me to help. So, I quickly changed into my chore clothes and headed to the other place, the adjoining farm my parents had bought. I got to the property and headed straight for where Dad was expected to be. I always liked to help with farm projects, so I arrived eager to help. Little did I know that the entire scenario had been meticulously prepared for my benefit. In the barn at the other place, there were tie stalls where, in years gone by, the workhorses were stabled, now a place to deposit all the baling twine after it had been removed from hay bales when feeding the sheep and cattle. I don't recall the project, but Dad instructed me to run into the barn and get him some baling twine, so I instantly headed to that first stall where the baling twine was always ready for the taking. I remember running into the barn and directly to the first stall and stopping in my tracks, staring at the object of my obsession and the first words out of my mouth, "Is he real?".

Little did I know, my parents followed me to the stall and responded, "Of course he is, and he is yours."

I know now that this is when my addiction to horses officially started.

There were a couple of prerequisites for my owning a horse. First, I had to complete my chores before I could ride him. Second, I had to ride him bareback as my parents could not afford a saddle for me. That was not a big problem as I had ridden my uncle's ponies bareback as well, so I had a good start. I recall it was winter when I received the pony, meaning I had school every day of the workweek. I was so horse crazy that I would set my alarm for 5 am, get up and have a cup of coffee with my dad, get dressed, and ride my pony for an hour before returning to the house to get ready to go to school.

This was my new everyday routine, and it seemed a perfectly normal addition to my fabulous new life. I recall riding on the range, our farm, chasing bad guys, imaginary, of course, all with the aid of "Flash," my wonder horse.

In the neighborhood I grew up in, a large farming operation raised corn, beans, and hay and used the harvest to finish cattle in their feedlot. In the fall, they would generally turn the cattle out onto the fields to feed on the corn stalks and grain and glean the fields of corn that may have been missed during the harvesting operation.

Being the new sheriff of the range, seeing cattle in a recently harvested cornfield across the road from our farm instantly made me realize I needed to act. Seeing that the gates to the field were open would allow the cattle to get out on the road. My cowboy senses kicked into high alert, knowing it was my job to mount my trusty steed and ensure the cattle did not wander onto the road. I rode my bicycle to the barn as fast as my little legs would pedal, threw a bridle on Flash, and rode hard and fast to save the community. In no time at all, Flash and I were in high gear to save the community, past my house, around the corner of the "T" road down to the open gate and charged into the field towards the cattle facing the danger head-on. I was tough that day and on top of my game until I got about 50 yards from the cattle. At that point, I pulled Flash to an abrupt halt as I realized that Curly, the resident breeding bull, was dead ahead of me. Curly, in my eyes, was the world's largest and meanest bull that had ever lived. Now Curly was a large Charolais breeding bull known to be somewhat ill-tempered. There I sat on my wonder horse, staring into Curly's eyes as he lowered his head and began to paw the ground. My Roy Rogers persona shrunk to Chicken Little immediately; I promptly turned around and returned to my house as fast as my wonder horse could carry me.

I spent countless hours riding my pony and honing my skills in riding; weekends would find me riding five miles to a friend's house to ride with him as we played tag on horseback, riding up and down the hills and valleys of his family's gravel pit.

As years passed, I outgrew my wonder horse and sold him to a neighbor girl who rode him for three or four years. I was allowed to borrow a horse from a nearby family and rode her for a couple of years. I upgraded horses to improve my efforts in the show ring as I was constantly competing in gaming events during the summer months, speed events like barrel racing, spear the ring, ribbon race, pole bending, keyhole race, speed in action, and flag race, as well as taking part in 4-H and playing in broom polo matches. My love of horses continued, and dreams of life in the horse industry filled my mind. I desired to be a jockey and ride in the Kentucky Derby, but I continued to grow, and people my size were not jockey material. My next horse dream was to ride jumping horses and someday ride in the Grand National in Aintree, England, and even compete in the Olympics. Yep, you guessed it, that didn't happen either; I was never going to be able to afford a world-class German Warmblood, the type of horse required to compete in that level of horse competition. Despite my grand dreams not coming to fruition, I knew I was destined to be in the horse industry. I rode and showed horses actively; I was at a local horse show until 2 am the night before my high school graduation.

After graduation, I was still active in horse activities. Still, I was trying to find my way to become a contributing adult who was both financially sound and employed in a fulfilling occupation. I had several jobs, but none seemed to be what I thought would be my lifelong career.

After two years of trying the factory work and other options, I answered an ad looking for someone to be a stable hand. In simple terms, I was cleaning horse stalls. I was young and tough, knew how to work hard, and had considerable experience working with and around horses. I was fortunate enough to get that job, and three months into the job, the owner asked me if I would be interested in working the horses and starting young horses. Without a second of hesitation, I said yes.

I rode and trained Tennessee Walking Horses for that private stable for ten years. I was blessed to have some great horses in our string; we always had 2 or 3 mature horses that the owners rode regularly, and we showed them in regional shows. On top of that, we had a breeding program and raised between 2 and 4 foals each year, training them for performance classes throughout the Midwest. The owners had invested a great deal of money in their show horses and had several horses stabled in Tennessee, where they routinely would travel and show them at major events. I was fortunate enough to travel to the Tennessee stable, work hand in hand with those trainers, and learn the ins and outs of training and showing in the Tennessee Walking Horses industry. Training the young horses was challenging but rewarding and educational; I progressed to the point where I was allowed to show a weanling colt from our stable. The experience of showing in the World Championships in Shelbyville, TN, was terrific. Our entry placed 14th in the Weanling Stallion in Hand Championship class.

Training young horses for competition requires hours and hours of ground and saddle time and constant changes and adjustments in their shoeing adjustments as their training progresses. Many times, late in the training process, I learned that minimal adjustments in how the bridle fit could change things in the final fine-tuning of a show horse for competition. Our regular farrier was located 2 hours away, so he worked with me to teach me the art of changing shoes on the young horses in training, as the need to change and adjust the shoeing was as often required once a week, saving him driving 2 hours for single shoeing once a week.

This knowledge proved beneficial when I branched out into my own blacksmithing and horseshoeing business full-time after ten years as the head trainer. The work is physically demanding but extremely rewarding, and it has opened the door to more wonderful experiences in the horse industry.

I want to give you some background on my horse industry experience. Of course, I spent hundreds and hundreds of hours riding and competing on horses before taking my first full-time position at a stable. I spent ten years working full-time at a stable, during the first three months as a daily stall cleaner, feeding horses and grooming animals for the daily rides by the stable owners. After that first three months, I was promoted to the head trainer position, worked the show horses when the owners were absent, and began a training program for the young horses on the property. The barn was 286 feet long, with 15-10 x 10 stalls and 2-10 x 20 foaling stalls with built-in creep feeders. Every year, we averaged 3-4 new young horses into the training program. We also averaged 3-5 aged show horses in conditioning full time, so we usually had 7-8 horses to work or train five days a week. The owners usually rode in the morning on Saturday, and I tried to have them completely cooled down and get them back in their stalls by noon.

As I stated earlier, I could travel back and forth to Tennessee and work with the top training stable for amateur riders. Being at this top-notch training facility allowed me to work with the industry's top-ranking Tennessee Walking Horses, many with multiple world titles. Some of the horses at the stable were as follows: Hills Perfection, Mr. Delight H, Call of the Wild, Delights Adonis, Mr. Wilson's Major, Star of the Show, Centennial Delight, Prides Gold Coin. Along with the great horses, I also had the opportunity to meet celebrities and business owners. There was never a lack of world championship-calibre horses to work with and ride; the four above-listed horses were owned by the stable where I worked. I was blessed to be able to work with and learn from top horse training facilities to build my horse resume.

Following my tenure at the training stable, I branched off into full-time blacksmithing in north central Indiana. I worked with a wide variety of horse breeds: Quarter Horse, Clydesdale, Belgian, Standard Bred, Hackney, Paso Fino, Shetland Ponies, American Saddlebreds, and Arabians, as well as a multitude of grade horses. My years of experience in training horses gave me excellent credentials for shoeing a variety of breeds and multiple riding disciplines. I assisted my customers in getting the proper movement, which is essential to successfully showing various disciplines and breeds. I have met and built incredible relationships with owners and trainers in my area. All the years of horse experiences with different breeds, meeting various horse owners, and collaborating with trainers laid the foundation to embark on my amazing equine adventure.

Chapter 2
Wheels are Set in Motion

It was early 1983, a beautiful spring day in northern Indiana. Trees were busting out with leaves, hay fields were perking up, farmers were tilling the ground, getting ready to plant seeds, and Mother Nature was putting forth the next generation. I was on my way to a customer's farm to do the first round of trimming of their herd of horses. As was customary, I worked in the pasture where broodmares and foals were grazing. My protocol for trimming a customer's brood stock was to trim the mare's hooves and then trim the foal at no charge. This was my idea of job security; going through the motions of trimming meant handling the foals, a way to ensure the youngsters got the early exposure, and by the time they became weanlings, they would have a relatively good start of having their legs handled. I was young and tough and capable of going toe-to-toe with any horse they threw at me, but I also knew that if I had taken care of the proper groundwork, life down the road might have made my experiences in future trimmings much easier.

One of the brood mares, a purebred Arabian, on the list, was Calamus, a grey flea-bitten mare with a foal at her side that had been born a few weeks earlier, March 21, 1983, to be exact. A flea-bitten (exceptionally light grey, with minor red tick marks of hair over the entire coat) would not score high on my list of want-to-own colors, but then again, pretty is what pretty does.

Alongside Callie was a darling foal, a bay, with three white stockings and a star, strip, and a snip. (reddish brown with black tail, mane, tips of the ears, as well as black from the knees down, provided they did not have white stockings) he was quite a looker. I began my trimming tasks on Callie as usual. I started with one of her front feet, picking it up, pulling it up between my legs just above my knees, and trimming. I had barely begun when this curious young foal decided he needed to come and investigate this procedure. The foal walked up to me as I was trimming and reached out, grabbed my cap by the bill, pulled it from my head, turned and walked twenty feet carrying it, and dropped it to the ground.

Upon completing the foot, I released it to the ground, walked over, and placed the cap back on my head. I considered it a unique introduction to a new future client. Once I picked up my cap from the ground, I returned to my trimming duties on the mare, picking up the rear leg on the same side I had completed the front foot a little earlier. Once again, I started on the rear foot; moments later, our bold little fellow walked up, grabbed the cap from my head, walked off twenty feet, and again dropped the cap. I once again walked over, retrieved my cap, and placed it on my head. I proceeded to trim the mare's other front foot; the persistent youngster once again came forward and stole the cap from my head, walked the twenty feet, and dropped the cap again on the ground!

By this time, all those present were laughing like crazy, and this bold young fellow was doing an excellent job of entertaining the crowd. Upon releasing the front leg, I again retrieved my cap. Not chewed, not stomped into the ground, just dropped from his mouth. I continued to finish the trimming of the mare, and true to form, once I had the final leg lifted and supported, I had a cap neatly removed from my head, carried the appropriate distance, and dropped it to the ground. True to form, no chewing, no stomping, just dropped to the ground, forgotten until the next opportunity to remove it from my head.

At the time, I saw him as a curious youngster investigating the strange new world he resided in and had new things to learn and discover. With what I had just experienced, I was sure this little fellow would make it in this world, no matter where he might find himself.

Time went on, and yes, as is typical in the horse world, I was requested to make a return trip to Blue Diamond Arabians to care for the feet of the herd. Yes, Callie was once again on the list to be trimmed. When her turn came around, she again was followed by a handsome and growing bay foal with three white stockings and a star, strip, and snip. By this point, he was three months old or a bit more and, in that time, had grown considerably. I began trimming the mare, and just as the first time, while starting on each foot, he would walk over, grab the cap, walk back a little distance, drop my cap to the ground, and stand there and wait. Each time I would drop the foot I had been working on, I would walk over and pick up my cap, place it on my head, and return to performing the assigned duties.

The farm was a regular customer, and I serviced their horses regularly. This charming young fellow continued to grow physically and in presence and confidence. This little activity he began on the first visit continued until his weaning. I remember one of the latter times visiting the farm; he performed his steal-a-cap routine as I trimmed his mother's hooves. Once I had finished the final hoof trimming, I walked over to retrieve my cap for the final time on that visit as he stood about 2 feet away from me. I shook my finger in his face and told him jokingly that if he kept this activity up, I was going to buy him and work his butt off.

Time passed, and I continued my visit to the farm and saw him regularly; with each visit, I saw the changes in his physical growth, dashing appearance, and most definitely bold but gentle presence; his "Look at Me" attitude kept speaking louder and louder. Visits continued through the summer of 1984 and 1985, and he matured into a unique, beautiful stallion with exquisite movement and a kind and desire-to-please attitude.

The fall of 1986 profoundly affected my future, not only on myself but also on one very striking young Arabian stallion who kept telling me that he was destined to be a part of my life from now until ever. This would be a unique experience as I was not prepared for what was in my future or his, but the writing was on the wall, and I knew he was meant to be a part of my life.

Chapter 3
School Begins

November 1986 finds me having made an offer to Blue Diamond Arabians for a 3-year-old purebred Arabian stallion. Yes, you guessed it, it was the beautiful cherry bay stallion with three white stockings, a star, strip, and snip with a beautiful heart, and the presence of a champion along with the ability to steal the cap off the head of a farrier. He was foaled on March 21, 1983, sired by Stone Arc Quedi, a bay purebred Arabian of Silverdrift lineage and other Egyptian bloodlines. On the damn side, he was the Grandson of Aramus; this horse was the first Champion of both the Canadian National as well as the U.S. National Arabian Association, owned by Mr. Wayne Newton, the famous Las Vegas performer who was heavily involved in the Arabian Horse Industry. This is the heritage of my new horse, Diamond Amus, affectionately known in the barn as Amos.

I had arranged to have him delivered to my farm in mid-December. The timing could not have been worse. I had the barn prepared to house him, but that was the only right thing. I had injured my back, was in a great deal of pain, and had minimal mobility. Amos arrived in mid-December, yelling and screaming his disapproval of the significant move. Since I was so disabled, I had to have my wife take care of this terrorized young stallion. The bad part of that was the fact that she was far from being an experienced horse handler. However, somehow, we survived the arrival, and the wife had to tend to his needs for a few days, but it needed to be resolved at once, or the wife would be killing not only the new horse but myself since I could not care for him.

Knowing I was buying Amos, I had already had a plan but had not yet confirmed the arrival of the new horse. I have already spoken with a client about doing the basic groundwork with Amos. I called the client I had arranged to come to my farm, pick up Amos, and take him to her farm, where she would begin the work on my horse.

Although new to horse training, I had seen her work and the results over the past couple of years and was sure she could perform the needed basic training to prepare him for the next level of his equine education.

We had planned to have Amos at Leslie's farm for about 60 days. Leslie was expected to teach Amos how to behave when being led in a halter and teach him to lounge (working in a circle on a 30-foot lounge line) where he would travel in a specific gait (walk, trot, lope) at a controlled speed, performing the gaits upon verbal command, being tacked up (saddle being applied), long-lined (driving from the ground) learning to turn in both directions, stop and back up. As mentioned earlier, all the training is a precursor to climbing in the saddle and riding. Unlike the cowboys on TV jumping on a horse's back and riding the buck out of them, I prefer training the horse slowly and building trust to avoid the horse ever learning how to buck.

By the end of the first 30 days, due to Leslie's talent and the honest desire to please and learn, Amos had made fantastic progress. Amos could lounge in both directions, responding correctly to the verbal commands to walk, trot, stop, and back. After two more weeks in the training program, Amos was found working under the saddle and following verbal and physical cues to walk, stop, and turn in both directions. Amos has exceeded expectations thus far, and it was time to move to the next training phase.

Chapter 4
School of Higher Education

The time had come to advance to Amos' next level of education. That next step was to transfer Amos to the care of Teresa Stutz, the head trainer at Wedgewood Walk Arabians. The facility is owned by Terri's sister, Judy, another client of my horseshoeing business. This facility had an incredible inside arena and many stalls for boarding horses and grassy paddocks to be turned outside in nice weather to blow off steam and enjoy nibbling on grass. There were crossties (standing stalls with the horse secured on both sides to the halter) for tacking and washing horses and nearby tack rooms. This was a genuinely nice facility. It catered to the boarding and training of horses and giving riding instruction. Perfect for year-round riding and training, which is necessary to be competitive in the Arabian show horse world.

The plan for Amos was to begin work under Terri's tutelage to train in the discipline of English pleasure. This choice was because I had regularly seen Amos in the pasture field where he was raised, trotting in a highly animated gait (trotting with his knees breaking above level). The ability of Amos to trot so big was one of the reasons I had an interest in him. When I watched him traveling across the green pasture, his mane flowing in the wind, his syncopated steps, and the bright white stocking was indeed a vision to behold. I pictured him in the show arena and was sure he could conquer the world. All I had experienced of him as a youngster made me believe he was special. He had what was referred to as "Presence," not unlike what top-caliber actors bring to the stage when performing in front of large crowds. Amos possessed a genuine "LOOK AT ME" attitude, with a kind heart and desire to please.

Terri's tasks were to take his talent and raw abilities and hone them. Teach him to obtain a specific gait and keep that gait with a particular cue from the rider, and to keep that gait until asked to do another gait. The idea is to perfect each step he takes and consistently perform it that way every time it is requested. This by no means is a simple task and takes hours and hours of saddle time, which requires consistent perfection from the trainer, making the cue and the action synchronized and invisible to the viewer.

Terri's protocol for saddleback training always began in western tack, even though the goal was to have him be an English horse (perform in English attire). The saddle Amos was to wear was not a concern, although Terri asked if I was okay with the choice since I was the owner. Having spent so many years training myself, I knew the horse would not be hindered from doing what was needed at the beginning of his training.

Terri began riding him five days a week, granting him weekends off to relax and be a horse. They logged many hours working on cues, gaits, suppleness in the mouth (supporting control through the bit with extremely light pressure), executing speed control while executing changes of direction with invisible cues, and keeping his body in the proper position. Terri quickly discovered that Amos could swallow his tail, invert his body, and be standing facing the opposite direction in a split second; nothing vile in his decision to do this, no violent bucking, rearing, or defiance exhibited, just excellent agility and body control, just to be facing the opposite direction, and to cause the rider to say, where did that come from? Yes, we discovered he was an incredible athlete because of the hours spent transforming his mind and body. The former round, somewhat plump body was transformed into a chiseled work of natural art. I constantly contacted Terri throughout this project and would visit her and her understudy regularly.

Amos was an exceptional student with a love for work, a talent exceeding my wildest dreams, a loving, kind heart, and a love for people. I discovered he, indeed, was as good of a horse as I had imagined him to be. However, one major problem presented itself: Terri's extreme talent could not get past it. If Amos were to be turned loose in the indoor arena, his athleticism would be incredible. He bolted across the arena as hard as he could and was instantaneously going in the opposite direction without any steps to the side to make a turn. He would raise his head, lift his tail, and break in an awe-inspiring highly syncopated cadence to his trot, and stylishly waving his raised head from side to side like a flag gently waving in the wind, his nostrils flared, snorting loudly as if to alert anyone to the fact they should be watching him. I would watch him perform and stare in awe at this incredible motion, his presence appearing wild and crazy but controlled and presented with flare and authority. I could not believe this was my horse. I was lucky to have found him.

Our problem was that with all his excellent movements while free in the arena, they would not come out while he was under saddle. His trot was rhythmic and fluid, rolling forward, but it was not bold and syncopated enough to be awe-inspiring in the English discipline. I have to say I was somewhat surprised by the news when Terri told me, yet somehow, I was far from being devastated. Terri told me she thought it best to concentrate our efforts on grooming him for Western pleasure. Although we were less than 30 days into his formal training, we knew he would not be the English horse I bought him for, but the horse trainer in me knew it was imperative to allow the horse to be the best at whatever he could be. I knew all horses were not World Champion Performance horses in OUR desired discipline. Our jobs as owners and trainers were to take the horse's natural ability and mold it into what best suits him, not necessarily what we want him to do. Teri quickly began steering Amos into Western pleasure discipline. Occasionally, I would stop by the stable and catch Terri putting Amos through his practice sessions, climb aboard, and do a lap around the arena. This is where I discovered that Amos, a mere 14.2 hands (a hand being 4" and measured to the top of the withers from the ground), felt more like a 16-hand horse. I was accustomed to working with much taller horses, which I was very fond of. It was not like I thought he was a little horse; he was similar in size to most Arabians of the era. However, newly discovered bloodlines were beginning to enter the market and producing taller and more streamlined Arabians.

The reformed training program continued with Amos, and progress was steady. His natural ability was showing, along with his desire to please and work on his assigned tasks. The hours of concentrated training were molding Amos into a more beautiful specimen than ever.

We were now into about 45 days of the second phase of his training program, so roughly mid-April, which placed us heavy into the shedding process of the horses and putting myself into getting busier and busier attending to the needs of my clients.

One day, I dropped into the stable to see how the student was progressing with the program, and Terri said she wanted to talk with me. She informed me Amos was doing quite well; she was amazed at how fast he had progressed, so she wanted to speak with me. Terri told me she thought we needed to consider getting Amos in a show to let us evaluate how he might react to crowds and the hustle and bustle of a horse show. My experience told me she was correct, as a horse show is a different environment with distractions in every direction; traveling with the horse too can upset their entire routine. A horse show can indeed be a game changer for young horses, and it is one that you never know how it will go until it happens. One will often believe it will be ok with only a minor bump in the road or two along the way, or it may turn the horse's world upside down. Either way, it was one of those things that all young horses need to experience if we intend to have a show horse. I informed Terri I was on board with the idea and told her to see what she might have available for us.

I was not in the least concerned about what would take place. I knew that horse shows in our area of northern Indiana are quite often available. Saddle clubs and breed clubs with various interests were available in our immediate area. I always called them Saturday night shows, small groups of people, a large variety of class choices, and enough activity to create a distraction and assess the nerves of a young horse to understand the tolerance level.

Three or four days later, I was again at the stable to visit Amos and Terri and see his progress, which was quite good. Terri informed me that she had found a show we should attend. My response was great; what did you find? I thought the most likely was a small show in Elkhart that the local Arabian Horse Club sponsored, commonly called the Wooly Show. This show was put together early enough in the year to give owners and riders a chance to get their horses into the show ring but not hold them to the significant show standards of the horse to be shed out entirely or need to be body clipped (clipping the entire body of the horse). This show was quite popular with the club members and locals and was often attended by very high-quality horses that were not necessarily ready for the bigger shows.

"I found a show that I think we should take Amos to, the Louisville All Arabian Classic horse show," Terri stated.

As I picked up my chin from the concrete floor of the horse barn alleyway, my mind was about to explode from what I had just heard.

"WHAT? Have you lost your entire mind? You must be nuts!"

Now, understand Terri and I are terrific friends, and I knew from the expression on her face that she was not surprised by my response. She had a smirk on her face, having already planned her rebuttal. Terri tried to tell me that she believed it would be a good test for Amos. I am pretty aware that this is a Class A All Arabian Show, but she felt confident that Amos was a good enough horse to make a respectable performance; she never said a word about the fact that she thought he could win anything. She felt he was ready to face the reality of the show-horse world.

Well, the formerly mentioned Wooly Show is held in a semi-rural location, with no physical stalls to board your horse; they would stand tied to the exterior of your trailer. There is no indoor arena, but ample room to take your horse to the outskirts of the show area to let your horse adapt to the noise and movements of constant activity.

Hearing the PA system at a distance is not as distracting or overwhelming at first. Hugely different from the Louisville Classic, which was held in a coliseum with hundreds of horses, and three times that in people, music playing on the PA system and an Announcer calling out gaits and directions over the PA system, the noise reverberating within the walls of the facility. Moreover, Amos had only been in training for less than four months. This was the last thing I expected to hear and the last thing I wanted to expose this new horse to. All I could imagine was an absolute disaster in the making. I've been there and done that on the trainer's end. I had the ultimate faith in my choice as a trainer, and although I was not overly excited about the choice of first shows, I had to follow my gut and her intuition to make this decision and continue to the next step. Ready or not, horse world, here we come.

Chapter 5
Ready or Not
Here We Come!

Well, all bets aside, we are on our way to the official introduction of Diamond Amus to the Arabian Horse World. I was facing this situation with excitement and trepidation, having limited experience with interaction with the Arabian Horse industry other than the trimming of their feet and the application of shoes and my contact with clients involved with Arabian Horses. Terri was busy putting all the information and documentation together that is required for a Class A (the top level of equine exhibition), which meant I would be required to obtain an Amateur Card from the Arabian Horse Association (governing body of Arabian Horses) which is necessary to exhibit Arabian horses to confirm you meet the qualification to show horses in specific classes and divisions.

The Louisville KY show was a 4-day event on Thursday, Friday, Saturday, and Sunday. Amos was entered into a class on the show's first day, and I could not attend the first day because of my commitment to clients. I will be arriving late in the evening on the first day of the show and scheduled to perform in a class on Friday. Knowing I would be able to show Amos for the first time was thrilling, but I needed to know every one of his buttons and be able to accomplish it without fault. I did not fear nor have a concern about going into the show ring, but I did need to hone my execution skills on the cues required to function as a single unit in the arena. Until now, Terri had been the primary rider, and Amos needed to become comfortable with me being at the controls, so I spent more and more time in the saddle with him. In a couple of weeks, we were operating like a fine-oiled machine, Amos doing precisely as instructed on command every time.

The trip to Louisville was a 5-hour drive from the stable location to the exhibition center and, fortunately, was safe and uneventful. The next day, Amos was scheduled to debut in the show arena, but I would not be there. The following day, I was up early to head to my scheduled appointment to service the client's horses, then on the road to Louisville for my first chance to perform in the arena with Amos. The day of trimming and shoeing horses was finally completed, and I returned home to shower, packed my bag, loaded my show clothes in the truck, and headed to Louisville.

The first item on the agenda when arriving in Louisville at the event was to locate the crew from our stable. I already had the stall assignment; it was just a matter of learning the facility's layout. I promptly found our stalls and contacted Terri; I was so anxious to hear about the class results she and Amos had been in. The first question out of my mouth was how it went. Terri, smiling, said pretty good, we placed 5th. Ok, you got a ribbon, but how did Amos do? She smiled an even more giant smile and said he worked perfectly, no issue whatsoever. We chatted more about the specifics of the class; they had participated in a 12-horse class performing in Western pleasure, Aged Stallions, which was most likely no other young inexperienced horses in the class. Hearing that Terri and Amos were up against 11 other contestants, I was feeling pretty good that Teri and Amos had made a pretty good representation of themselves, knowing it was inevitable this show was not drawing in the non-competitive stock; this caliber of this show will draw in the best in the area. I could not see my face, but I am sure I was smiling ear to ear, and I breathed a sigh of relief; the first hurdle was out of the way. Tomorrow, I will be put to the test along with Amos in that Western Pleasure Maiden Horse Class (Maiden means never having won a blue ribbon).

The following day, there was a flurry of activity in the stall area for our crew. Amos needed to be given a quick ride to make sure he was on top of his game, then a good bath, towel him dry, make sure his feet were picked out and there were no issues, paint his feet, powder his stockings, comb out his mane and tail, make sure the saddle and bridle are clean and shining. While completing all these activities, it was imperative to pay attention to how they were progressing on the show-ring side of things. All our preshow activities needed to be completed so we had time to get to the makeup arena and warm him up for his class.

The hard part was now completed, and we were in the makeup arena working through our warmup, walking, jogging, loping, stopping, setting him up for the judge to review, and backing. The makeup arena was busy with many horses preparing for classes, and before long, we heard the call for our selected class to enter the arena at a jog-trot, and Amos and I made our way into the show arena. My experience in showing kicked into gear, and I had positioned myself to be the first to enter the arena; many exhibitors do not want to be the first to enter. However, my experience taught me that being the first in the arena was an advantage. I see the advantage of entering the arena first for two good reasons, the first being you know the judge will see you and a first impression is a lasting impression; second, the first horse I see when I am judging is what I used to evaluate the rest of the entries. Once all the horses had entered the arena under the judge's eye, he had a good idea which horses were ligament contenders. The announcer called for the gate to be closed, and all the participants were in the arena and to work on the rail at a jog-trot. Amos and I complied with the instructions and soon heard the call for a walk on the rail, which we promptly slowed to the walk. While working in the arena, I tried to ensure I kept Amos as visible to the judge as possible, as this was a large class with 35 entries. Sometimes, I chose to work off the rail; rather than be covered up behind other exhibitors, I would guide Amos closer to the center of the arena to ensure maximum exposure to the judge. This was a new experience for Amos, as he was still learning, and most of the training was performed on the rail. But like the shining star that he was, he did everything just as if we were working on the rail like a well-seasoned show horse. The arena announcer called for a lope, and I gave Amos the cue to lope in the left lead. The transition was flawless, and his lope was smooth and steady. Having completed the loping to the left, the announcer called for the hand gallop (similar to a lope but faster).

Once again, I needed to concentrate on where all the other competitors were because of the speed involved. One could quickly get themselves into a bad situation. The announcement came for riders to work at a walk on the rail, and at the request, I brought Amos to a walk from our hand gallop and was thrilled at the beautiful transition I received from Amos. The request to reverse and walk came over the PA speakers, and Amos and I circled smoothly toward the center of the arena and headed down the rail for our work in the opposite direction. We were instructed to do a jog-trot on the rail, and having gone nearly two circuits of the arena, the request for a walk came over the speakers.

As before, the following request would be for a lope, and we were soon loping on the rail. Next came the instructions to hand gallop; once again, I did my best to expose Amos to the judge and not get run over by other exhibitors so we could pass and avoid horses with no issue. Lastly, we were instructed to walk, come in, and line up in the center of the arena. We turned into the center of the arena, lined up, set Amos up, and waited for the judge to make his way down the line of horses, asking each competitor to back their horse. Amos performed the reverse maneuver, returned to our original position, and waited for the judge to inspect the rest of the horses in the arena. While sitting in the arena, I reviewed the performance in my head, incredibly proud of how well he performed in the class. Before long, the PA speakers crackled, signaling an upcoming announcement, likely the results of the judge's evaluations, and they were about to announce the placings for this class of 35 maiden horses. The announcer called out, saying the entry number on my back, and called Diamond Amus the winner. We had just defeated a class of 34 other horses at our first horseshow and only the second class of his career; without a doubt, I could not have been happier with the performance of this young horse of mine.

I received our blue ribbon and the trophy and returned to the makeup arena, where we would reunite with our crew. I entered the makeup arena, turned left, and saw Terri walking toward us. I let out a war hoot as loud as possible while raising my hand and holding the trophy above my head. Only seconds after my glee of joy in the makeup arena, I heard the ring announcer say, "Somebody is Happy!"

An understatement as I was thrilled at what had just happened. Pulling Amos to a stop, I dismounted Amos and saw Terri Five feet in front of me with the biggest smile on her face. She walked up to Amos, gave him a good rubbing on his face, and told us what a fantastic job we both had done. Then she turned toward me, walked up, and wrapped her arms around me in a giant bear hug, immediately placing me into rigor mortis and my mind screaming, "Oh My God, Terri is Touching Me!". I must advise you that the response to Terri's hug has been brought up in many conversations since it occurred. Now, let's go back to the real story. This horse had been in training less than six months, and we had just defeated a class of 34 other contestants, his first time at a horse show. What we were experiencing here, this is not normal at all. I was beginning to see this little horse, which was everything I saw in him, and I was more than impressed with how he performed on this first of many outings to come. I feel confident that Amos has been in the arena a couple more times in Louisville. Still, in my euphoric state after such a big initial win, I don't recall any other results. I am thinking we are about to light this candle.

Chapter 6
Time to Light this Candle

The days following the Louisville Classic were quite exciting for me. The first horse show experience with Amos convinced several others he was something special and, for me, how much more special he indeed was. I had known for some time that Amos was unique; from that first meeting when he was just a few weeks old, there seemed to be a bond between us that I could not explain. I have been around horses nearly every day of my life, everything from ponies to some of the most expensive show horses of the era. But this was different; as much as I was smitten by the adorable foal when we first met and offered to purchase him, I knew deep down in my heart that he had chosen me, not the other way around. Some friends and acquaintances thought I had gone off the deep end. But I knew Amos and I had a special relationship; he loved people, loved to work, was a quick learner, and was very easy on the eyes; he was what I call the complete package. Above all else, he had personality and a sense of humor; little did we know we had only experienced a tiny glimpse at this point.

Terri was extremely excited with her new understudy and was almost as intoxicated with him as much as I was. She made it clear to me that we WERE going to continue working with him in the Western Pleasure discipline, which I knew was the right choice. She saw the wonders in this little horse, as I had told her. The results of that first show confirmed my belief that the show ring was his domain; his LOOK AT ME attitude was coming through loud and clear. The makeup arena was a different creature altogether.

The following experience at a horse show revealed some interesting things that surprised us all, and the Indianapolis Arabian show was our next target. I trusted Terri to pick and choose the shows we attended, as well as our class eligibility: Jr Horse (4 yrs. and under), Novice (having won no more than three blues), Men's Amateur, Stallion Open, Ladies were on the agenda for this show. The first glitch we discovered in human understanding of Amos was the importance of the down-and-roll maneuver. Again, I had commitments to customers and was not always at the shows as early as was required for some classes. The Indianapolis show found Terri showing Amos in the

Ladies' class and returning to the stall by winning the blue ribbon.

Back at home, following a good workout, Amos always received a refreshing shower, then, when nearly dry, he would be released into the arena where he would promptly lie down and roll, which is typical for most horses. What we did not understand is that in the case of Amos, it was not a privilege but a requirement. Following her win in the class, Terri returned to the stalls and was busy preparing other horses for classes. Later in the day, Terri was scheduled for another class with Amos and proceeded to the makeup arena for his warmup. Immediately, Terri started experiencing some attitude from Amos, in that he did not light up as had always been the case. She continued her warm-up routine to no avail, and his resistance did not end. She did not feel improper cadence while moving; it did not come across as a pain issue, and nothing that Terri could not seem to resolve the situation or get that "I am going in the show ring" response as had always been the case. Terri was not only concerned that there was a medical issue but stumped at what was happening. She knew the performance in the show ring would not be good if this continued. Terri reviewed in her mind anything that might be different, and then she remembered "the roll after a working," which she always allowed to happen after a workout, had not happened following the Ladies' class.

At lightning speed, Terri dismounted, and the staff stripped the tack from Amos, put a halter on him, and, with a lead rope, led him to a somewhat quiet area of the makeup arena. Amos immediately dropped to the ground and, with Terri holding the lead rope, allowed him to roll several times, stand, and shake. Now, with a dirty horse, they frantically brushed him to get the dirt off and the tack back on to get him presentable for the quickly approaching class. Once Terri returned to the saddle and proceeded with the warmup, Amos was happy as a lark. Go figure, I had a high-maintenance horse now. The class was called to the arena, and when the smoke and dust disappeared, Amos exited with a second-place ribbon in the Arabian Stallion Open class. That was a valuable lesson; although the makeup arena is not home, there better be a rolling session to reward performance. The lesson was learned and was never again an issue.

I arrived at the show grounds that evening following the arena rolling episode. It was pretty humorous to hear how ordinarily cool, calm and collected Terri was in panic mode, trying to figure out what was going wrong. I was pleased with the news of the first and second places in the classes. To this point, other than the 5th place in the Stallion class in Louisville, we were in the top two of every class we showed in, which, in my opinion and experience, is a pretty good place to be with such an inexperienced horse. I was no longer qualified to show in Maiden Horse classes; however, I was allowed to show Novice since our blue-ribbon tally was two and the limit was three or less. Tomorrow would be my second chance to show Amos, and I was thrilled at the opportunity that awaited me.

The following day finds us busy going about our duties of feeding and cleaning stalls, washing horses for the show ring, cleaning tack, and laughing about our privileged child requiring a roll in the dirt, which I must say was now an official task to be completed daily even at horse shows. I was getting my show clothes on while the rest of the crew did the final touch-up on Amos. As had been the case thus far, the walk to the makeup arena was noneventful, and we began our warmup; true to form, the warmup was flawless due to the addition of the dirt bath. I would be answering the call to the Novice class, and truthfully, I do not recall the number of horses in the class, but my estimate would be in the 30s. As was my usual approach, I set myself up to enter the arena first, at a jog trot as is normal, and the class began once all entries were in the arena. Upon the request for the first gait, it was attained instantaneously. The first thought in my mind is wow, Amos is getting incredibly responsive to his cues. Working the gaits in the first direction of the arena was as close to perfect from Amos as I could have asked; his response to the cues was swift. The announcer called for a reverse and walk on the rail, and we promptly complied. The following announcement for a gait change was mere heartbeats away as I distinctly heard the announcer's click on the microphone just before the request to jog-trot. Suddenly, I realized we were already transitioning to the jog-trot at the click of the microphone. The only thing that would have presented a problem was if the judge had looked at us at that precise moment. Because the class had a required gait order, Amos had already figured out the next move by clicking the microphone.

For the rest of the class, I listened like a hawk to the microphone to give the slightest tap to the reins to prevent Amos from entering Autopilot mode. We made it to the end of the class and stood quietly as the judge performed his backing inspection on each horse. Once the announcement began, I listened intently to his calling out My back number and naming Diamond

Amos as the class winner. Wow, two classes and two blue ribbons. I just eliminated the Novice Horse class from our list of classes we could show him. I also discovered that Amos was brilliant and now needed to put everyone on alert that he was anticipating every move in the arena.

Returning to the makeup arena, we found our crew again in high spirits. However, I did curb my enthusiasm and did not scream at the top of my lungs, and thankfully, Terri did not apply a bear hug. I guess the rigor mortise tipped her off because I was a little uneasy with it. Shortly after completing the Indianapolis show, we discovered another show-ring quirk. As is sometimes the case with any show ring performance, the results do not always come out as anticipated. I have my opinions of the situation, which may or may not be valid. But I do know for a fact that people, in general, have preferences.

I stated early in this book that I was not a fan of the flea-bitten coloration of a horse, nor am I a fan of the Appaloosa colorations, but the coloration has nothing to do with the quality of the horse. My experience in the show ring exhibiting and judging horses has assured me that judges have a preference. I am guilty of reviewing horse show flyers to see who the judge was. Over time, you learn who looks favorable on your horses and who does not; this alone can result in one choosing to attend a show or not. One show we attended did not give us the results we anticipated. The very first class of the show in which Terri was performing ended, and they stood in the final lineup waiting for results, and the microphone came to life. The announcer started in first place, and the blue ribbon went to some number she was not wearing; she was not overly concerned as she had seen second place many times. The announcer continued with second place and some numbers, which she was not wearing but stood in place awaiting the balance of the results. When the following announcement was completed, she still had not been called. At this point, Amos was ready to announce his objection to not being acknowledged. He began to fidget in the line, nothing too serious at first, but as the ribbons were continued being awarded, Amos continued letting the world know of his knowledge that an error had occurred; it never got to the point where dismissal from the arena was required, but it was no doubt in our minds he was not pleased.

All the experiences listed occurred in the first few months of his show career, and once we understood his thought process, the activities became simple to deal with in the main scheme of things. Our show career continued nonstop for the next few years, with continued success with a blue ribbon awarded in most of our classes and a reputation for being the horse to beat. As our reputation in the show ring was building, we lit the candle, and it was burning brightly; unbeknownst to me, a storm was brewing.

Chapter 7
A Storm is Brewing

We have had an incredible journey thus far, with remarkable results in the local area shows, the Arabian Horse circles, and all the Arabian shows we could attend. I could not have been more satisfied with how Amos turned out. He was an incredible athlete, as solid in his gaits as any horse I had ever ridden and shown. He was the most incredibly consistent and honest horse I have ever experienced.

We realized Amos knew what was required of him in the show ring, so much so that I often wondered if he could do the entire class with no rider. The fun part of showing him was knowing that if I asked for a left lead, a left lead would be what he delivered. He never delivered an incorrect lead in the show ring in all the years and classes we competed in. Now, I can't say the same about a makeup ring as he seemed to use the makeup ring as a playground for him to use as a stress reliever.

On numerous occasions, the warmup arena has had monster leaves attack but only on a windy day, or an individual talking with his hands who is mistakenly identified as a sword-wielding horse assassin, or maybe a hat-wearing gentleman standing close to the rail that is the headless horseman poised to attack, or the small tree branch which is a giant crevice in the surface of the earth that he was about to fall into. Although all those scenarios occurred in the makeup arena, the second the entry gate for the show ring opened, it was all business, and none of those items even presented a concern. Amos not only entertained our love for showing in the arena, but he entertained us in the makeup arena. He did provide excitement in the show ring, but that was throwing down the Gauntlet. This horse had undoubtedly given me great joy, starting long before he became mine. He generates so much pride in my life for having the grand opportunity to own him and the pleasure of working with such a fantastic creature of God's making.

But the future was not looking good for Amos or Myself. I had a severe injury which required emergency surgery on my back. As hard as I tried, I was losing the battle of recovery. I was constrained by mobility; the pain was constant. To add insult to injury, my attempt to change careers to avoid shoeing horses daily was not working out. My wife filed for divorce; I was in a constant state of depression, and I was not in a good place.

Unable to ride my prized possession, Amos, and with my finances going upside down, I knew I would no longer be able to maintain ownership of Amos. I could not allow a horse of Amos' caliber to vegetate in a stall and paddock, knowing how much he loved the showring. I had always had a pet peeve of horse people talking about how much they loved their horses, which were only lawn ornaments, and I could not do that to my beloved Amos. So, I advertised that Amos was for sale and needed to do it as quickly as possible. In just a few days, I received a call from a gentleman who told me he had years of horse experience and needed a good horse for his 9-year-old daughter to show. Arrangements were made for them to come to my house and meet Amos. The visit started with meeting Amos over the corral fence and then asking if they could ride him, so the saddle came out, and with the assistance of the father, Amos was quickly prepared for a test ride. I explained his controls and advised him that he was a safe and trustworthy mount. The father assured me his daughter was highly experienced and stated he had no concerns about her ability. The test drive went very well for the most part until she stopped

Amos in front of her father and me on one of the passes. After a short chit-chat session with her father, he instructed his daughter to kick him and see if he could run. I remarked that would not be a good idea and that he did not need a kick to get him to run, just a firm squeeze. The father insisted he needed to see his daughter run. At that moment, the daughter applied the encouragement to proceed forward, true to the nature of "Ask, and Thou Shalt Receive", Amos launched. The daughter was jolted back and to the left, and Amos squirted right out from under her. The daughter got up from the ground, shaken but not stirred, and promptly responded to her father, saying yes, he can run, Dad. They appeared so happy with their inspection of Amos and sounded as if they appreciated what he had accomplished in his career thus far. They spoke of the desire to show him in 4-H and local shows. I felt he was going to a good home where he would be well cared for and appreciated for his desire to please. A week later, they arrived with a trailer to haul Amos home, and it was one of the saddest days of my life; I felt like I had turned my back on the dearest friend I had ever known.

Chapter 8
Redemption At Last

Many years had passed, 10 to be precise, since I had parted ways with an incredible horse I dearly loved. I thought of Amos many times over those years; I had considered searching for him but could not follow through, fearful of what I would find out. Many changes had occurred over those ten years: my children had grown and were now living on their own, I had met a woman after being single for some years, I had moved to a different area of the State of Indiana, I was successful in my new career working for the railroad as a locomotive engineer, and best of all I had undergone a second surgery on my back. Due to improvements in medical techniques, the second surgery gave me relief from the pain and allowed me to be able to resume many of the activities that I had been unable to enjoy for years.

Michelle, my new wife, came into my life; it was a package deal; she had three grown children. Her eldest son had been in the U.S. Army and now lives in Germany, where he had served. He stayed in Germany following his discharge to stay with his girlfriend,

Diana. Conversation with Diana included horses she dearly loved and had experience with. The conversation also led to their return to the U.S. to meet the prospective new in-laws. The conversations continued, and we spoke a great deal about horses, so we arranged some horse time for Diana during her visit. I had been removed from the horse circle for many years and needed to contact some residents to see if we could arrange something. It turned out to be relatively easy to find horse people in the area. The conversations with my wife brought up the fact that she had an interest in horses that I never knew about.

All the talk of horses and planning horse activities for the would-be daughter-in-law triggered some long-suppressed thoughts about Amos. So much so that I began having dreams about Amos, an extremely vivid dream that continued to reoccur. I shared this dream with Michelle, and she was insistent upon me pursuing the dream, as she had heard me speak of Amos many times. The dream saw me looking for and finding my long-lost friend after all these years. In my heart, I was very doubtful that this would even be possible, let alone be positive news. About a week later, I was not working due to the training program I was working on with the railroad. On the first day off work, Michelle said we should look for Amos; with little or nothing to go on, the search began.

I did not have much to go on to begin the search. I knew the name of the gentleman I had sold Amos to, and I remembered the name of the town where he had lived, but that was ten years ago. The first step was for me to dig out the phone book, search for the town name, and then search for the fellow's name. I was shocked to find his name in the phone book and more shocked to discover it was only about a 45-minute drive from where we lived. I called the number, but there was no answer, and I could not leave a message. Michelle said we had an address and that we should drive there and see if we could find the house. The road trip started, and about an hour later, we found the address and went by, visually searching the property for any sign of Amos, but to no avail. We drove back to the house, and I walked to the door, knocked, and waited for an answer. With no response, I turned and headed for the car to get in and leave. As I opened the car door, I heard a voice and turned to see an older gentleman standing on the porch calling to me. I returned to the porch and introduced myself, saying I was looking for the individual's name as I had remembered. He responded yes, that is me, so I immediately asked if Amos was there. His response came in a prolonged response, with a powerful aroma of alcohol in the gentleman's breath, no, and my hopes immediately shattered, knowing that finding Amos would not happen. There was another lengthy pause, then a response saying he was on loan to a friend to be company for the friend's horse. His daughter had gotten married, had an infant, and did not have time for a horse. He then told me to hold on a minute, entered the house, and returned a few minutes later, saying he called the family that was boarding Amos, but nobody answered the phone, but if we were willing to drive, he would take us to the location, and I could see Amos. He informed me that it was only about 25 minutes away, and I said that would be great. I was elated; I was going to get to see Amos again. Against all the odds, I had found my beloved friend and was going to see the long-lost friend I had parted with years before.

The drive seemed to last forever with all my anticipation of the reunion. The drive finally ended, and I scanned the property for my Amos but did not see him. The owner led us down a small path surrounded by waist-high weeds, multiple piles of trash, and highly run-down fencing, certainly not horse-worthy by any stretch of the imagination. I was beginning to get concerned about what I was going to find. A few minutes later, my eye landed on a familiar form: AMOS! I entered the paddock, filled with dried weeds, standing nearly chest high and scattered among the tall, dried weeds. Nothing but coarse weeds were growing sparsely on the ground without any visible grass. Amos, the once muscular, stately steed, was not reduced to a skinny, dull-coated horse, evidence of bites and scratches from conflict with other horses in multiple locations, standing there cowering, appearing very emotionally deflated; there was no sparkle in his eyes as I had remembered. I was devastated by his body condition, as well as the terrible environment that he had been forced to endure. I felt I had indeed failed Amos, selling him to a family with no idea what they had. As I stroked his neck and rubbed his muzzle, I told him how sorry I was for what I had done to him, selling him to these people.

About 15 minutes into my reunion, the property owners returned, and shortly after that, the owner asked me if I would like to ride Amos; I answered a resounding yes, and they offered to allow Michelle to ride the Mustang mare they also had on the property so she could go with me. We saddled up the horses, and while doing so, they told stories about how Amos would not do this or do some other thing, one being that he would not walk on the concrete platform from an old building in his paddock. All this talk was rubbing me the wrong way, as I knew far too well what this horse had accomplished in the past, and I took the remark about the concrete as a challenge. Michelle and I had a pleasant ride for about 20 minutes, and I was elated to share this time with Amos and have Michelle meet him. As we rode, I explained to Michelle that because Amos would not go on the concrete, it only proved these people had no credible horse knowledge and skill. As I returned from our ride, I turned toward the concrete pad and directed Amos up onto the concrete without the slightest form of a refusal for him. I was happy to see the owner and the property owners standing there in awe at the simple demonstration I had just performed. After all those years, Amos still responded to me as if he had always been with me. We finished our ride and began stripping the horses; once completed, we headed for the car to return home.

I was on cloud 9, thanks to Michelle pushing me to pursue the dream I had experienced, to follow through, and to have a reunion with my dear friend. Although I was saddened by the body condition I witnessed, the deplorable conditions he was being housed in, and the apparent lack of sparkle in his eyes, I was much relieved to see he was alive. As we drove to the owner's house, he began to talk of his daughter and her lack of time for Amos; he also told of how he had been in a severe automobile accident a few years earlier and then stated Amos was for sale. No doubt, trying to plant the seed that we should buy him would not be the case as a horse would not fit into our lives as we lived on the lake, not on a farm where he needed to be housed. It just was not an option for us.

Chapter 9
The Horse World Through the Eyes of Michelle

Authors Note: My wife, Michelle, penned this book section 8 years after her introduction to Amos. The reader deserves background to understand how and why she responds in this section. First, the purchase of Amos was an act of unselfish love towards me, her husband. Michelle had only ridden a pony a few times; she was in no way, shape, or form an experienced horse rider, but she did like horses a great deal. Stories of Amos had bombarded Michelle: what he achieved in the show ring, his love for people, his willingness to please, and his quirky little actions. Michelle did not learn to ride until she was in her mid-forties, and, honestly, she was clueless when walking headfirst into this situation. Her knowledge of all things equine was that they eat grain and hay, create tons of fertilizer, and you sit on their backs, and they walk you around.

Michelle

I could not believe we had found Jim's old horse. All the stories he had told me about this animal, how wonderful and unique he was, and the most beautiful thing you had ever seen. Jim was distraught with the condition we found him in; his hooves flared, needing the attention of a farrier. His ribs, showing from lack of adequate feed, and appearing to have lost his zeal for life, he seemed depressed. I could not see the animal he remembered; there was nothing special about this animal. I saw nothing but a rundown old horse; how ignorant I was. Jim kept telling me that purchasing him back was my decision alone and that I should only repurchase him if I wanted him. I could see this old horse was just what I needed and wanted because I still did not know how to ride. I told Jim I needed to go back and ride him for myself before deciding. But honestly, I had already decided to repurchase him, not for myself but for Jim; he loved this old bag of bones. I did not know why, but he did.

Jim planned for me to return and ride Amos this time. Once we arrived, Amos was saddled for the test ride; I crawled on and asked him to move, which required a firm boot in the ribs to get a trot out of him. I had to kick even harder to get him to lope and continued kicking to keep him loping; it was slow, like slow motion. No problem, I could ride this horse and be good at it with little effort, or so I thought. I agreed to purchase Amos; now, we had to find a place to board him, locate someone to haul him to his new home, and buy the equipment required to ride him. Reality hits hard, even harder when you think you have already figured it out. The day of the arrival of Amos was exciting for both Jim and me, except for Jim; it was good, but for me, it was terrifying. Jim was home, and he helped unload him; we decided we should have a little ride. We pulled out the new equipment, and Jim helped me get all the equipment appropriately fitted and adjusted for my size; Amos stood there, never moving a muscle through the entire process.

I climbed on him, and he began to dance around, acting like a 3-year-old with ants in their pants, and could not wait to get going. To put it mildly, he was scaring me, and with each move, the fear traumatized me even more; I was sitting astride Freddy Kruger of the equine world. I finally got him to stop long enough for me to dismount and Jim to climb aboard and take him for a ride; he said it was the Amos of old times, ready, willing, and able. I think we had gotten Jim a horse, but what about me? I was supposed to be getting a horse. I quickly realized that I could not manage this beast the way I was riding, or rather the way I was sitting on a horse. Amos was very high-spirited and much more horse than I expected, and with my lack of experience in my horse career, I was in over my head. I attempted to ride him again, and Jim kept telling me Amos would not hurt me and to keep trying. I just wanted to walk around; that was my comfort zone. I wanted a slow, easy, controlled walk, like when I first rode him.

At first, Amos was a mere hop, skip, and jump down the road from our house, boarded by a family with a young daughter who also loved horses. I had to learn to lead, brush, and saddle the horse to ride. I would visit Amos daily, with lots of brushing and petting, because that was the safest interaction. Jim's job required him to be gone from home often, sometimes multiple days at a time. I could saddle the horse, put the bridle on him, crawl on, and do what I thought was riding. Jim encouraged me to keep trying, as Amos would never hurt me.

A few months later, Amos was relocated to an actual horse farm just outside our small town. I rode daily, attempting to maintain a slow, meandering speed, MY comfort zone. Amos, the old horse, was here saying, Let's go; what is wrong with you? I had never seriously trotted or loped a horse, let alone hand-gallop. The stable where Amos was staying was an old racehorse farm, and the area we usually rode was the remains of the track used to exercise and train the racehorses. We would walk around the track and sometimes trot. The day finally arrived when Amos could no longer tolerate the Granny Gait I desired. He began his audition for the Kentucky Derby, the Grand National Steeple Chase, and the Indianapolis 500 all in one. I was scared stiff, frozen in the saddle; I did not know what to do with an animal hell-bent on running away. He did not run across the road or bolt through the open fields but stuck strictly to the route we usually rode around the old track. But instead of a slow, controlled walk that was my comfort zone, he let it all hang out, all or nothing. I do have to give him credit for slowing down for the corners to ensure I did not fall off; there was no zigzagging, no bucking; I felt out of control and indeed was. When we arrived back at our starting point, he gently eased his speed until he stopped, took a massive breath of air, and exhaled as if to say, "Boy, did that feel good. I told Jim about the behavior, and he was stunned. But Amos was calm about it; he never did any of that when Jim was around, making me appear a fool. I had gotten to the point where I was too scared to crawl on him anymore; I wanted nothing to do with this animal anymore; he was too much for me to deal with.

Jim felt it was time to get me professional help as he was not around enough to be able to solve our problems. He told me to call Terri, the person who initially trained him. I called and called and called yet again, but I could not get as much as a return phone call. He assured me I would be fine once Teri tuned him up and returned him to his proper show condition. YEAH RIGHT! Jim finally got to call Terri, and she promptly returned his call. I felt like I was not even being considered in this operation, not getting a response from Terri. However, as communications went on, we learned much information regarding what had transpired after Jim's sale of Amos 10 years earlier.

Terri reported to us she witnessed an episode of Amos being exhibited at a show she was attending, apparently following the class not having won; shortly after exiting the arena, the former owner's daughter began jerking violently on his mouth and batting him on the top of the head. Witnessing this action so upset Terri, she quickly returned to the barn where her horses were located, walked into the tack room, and cried uncontrollably from the abuse she witnessed. You see,

Terri was as big of a fan of Amos as Jim. She also informed us that she did not return my call because she thought someone was trying to play a mean trick on her. After all, the former owner's daughter's name was also Michelle, and their last name was the same as ours. This fact caused a couple of issues later in this chapter. Despite her overbooked schedule, Terri agreed to take Amos, tune him up, and give me lessons so I could learn how to ride him. She would do anything for this unruly horse; I didn't know why, at least not yet.

We loaded Amos in a trailer and hauled him just over 1-hour drive away to get him started. We had learned from the previous owners that he had not been shown or even worked regularly for at least the past 3 or 4 years. Terri greeted her long-lost friend, tacked him up, and headed for the arena, stopping after about 15 minutes and saying she believed she would need about 60 days to get him back to his show-performing status. Then, I could begin to take lessons and learn precisely how to control and ride him.

Two weeks later, Terri contacted us, stating that by the conclusion of the first 30 days, Amos would be ready for me to start taking lessons. Terri tried to convince me that I should start taking lessons on one of the school horses rather than Amos. I told her Amos was my horse, and if I were going to ride him, I would take lessons on him. As the lessons progressed and the bond between Terri and myself grew, we became very close friends; Terri eventually told me that the suggestion of riding a school horse was due to the fact she was afraid I was going to hurt Amos due to my inexperience, she was only trying to protect Amos. Imagine that, protect the horse from ME; I was the one on this evil creature that had attempted to kill me on numerous occasions; I was the one scared to death.

Terri knew my concern about crawling back into the saddle and what he had been exposed to after Jim sold him. I knew I had to do this right because if I did anything to hurt Amos, Terri would have hit the roof, and Jim would have forced me to take lessons on another horse. With all this, I still could not understand why they thought so much of this horse; he had done nothing but cause me grief. We hauled Amos back home and determined to ride him; I crawled back on. I felt like I was on a time bomb waiting for the explosion. Amos would collect himself and act so full of life, and if I shifted in the saddle, he would get antsy, wanting to do something.

Later, I learned I was giving him cues, so we decided to stop riding until the lessons started the next week. Until then, we would have bonding time, grooming, and treats—lots of treats.

The lessons started in earnest in January, hauling Amos to Terri's once a week for an hour lesson; at home, 3-4 days a week, I would work him at the barn where he was boarded, working on things Terri taught me in the most recent lesson. Amos would get antsy, but it was beginning to scare me less and less. From what Terri experienced seeing him at shows, we figured Amos concluded that if he ran, the rider would be busy trying to get him stopped rather than beat on him. Proof positive the best defense is to have a good offense.

One of the strangest situations we discovered was Amos' reaction when Terri would call me by my name while giving me directions during lessons. Since the previous owner's name was also Michelle, and she had not treated him well, he even reacted to the calling out of my name. It was three months before Amos quit reacting adversely to my name being used. He was learning that not every Michelle would hurt him, and Terri could call me by my name and not cause a reaction. I also knew I could not tense up when things went sideways and did not react with panic when I was uncomfortable. I was getting to where I could maintain a calm attitude and not send my uneasiness to Amos. I learned that my emotional status set the stage for how things went. I had to keep my body tension in check regardless of when my mind was screaming as loudly as possible.

I worked hard trying to absorb all Terri was teaching me, and when at home, working hours and hours trying to perfect my actions to get the most out of lessons. Jim and Terri had heard me mention I was interested in taking him into the show ring and told me it would likely be a year before I was ready for that. I am one of those highly competitive people and telling me it would be a year was like waving a red cape in front of a fighting bull. I took that as a challenge and worked harder to get where I could ride Amos in the show ring. I would practice keeping good posture while in the saddle and giving the correct cues. When at work or home and not riding, I would practice giving cues when I sat in a chair and drove the car. I would show Jim and Terri, and it would not take me a year to make it into the show ring. At home, I kept hearing how Amos and Jim did this and did that in the show ring. Again, all that talk made me more determined to work harder and prove myself so Amos and I could be right up there. I WAS GOING TO SHOW THEM!

March arrived, and I was invited to a mock bomb training seminar with Terri. I had been working very hard and could walk and jogtrot with confidence. I figured the workshop would be a good thing to push my skills, build my confidence, and help Amos and me bond and build a stronger relationship. I hauled Amos to Terri's barn, loaded her horse, and continued our road trip to bomb training. Once at the facility where the training was to take place, we tacked up the horses and headed for the barn to get the horses warmed up for the seminar and give me a chance to get used to the new surroundings. The first obstacle was to walk our horses over a mock wooden bridge that felt and sounded like an actual bridge. The program was set up in a follow-the-leader style with an experienced horse in the lead to help an inexperienced horse see and encourage them to follow the horse in front of them. In two attempts, I completed the first task without Amos jumping off the side of the bridge. OK, no sweat, I think. Obstacle number two is the same bridge, but they have installed a 4 X 4 under the center, so now it teeters when the horse reaches the center of the bridge. It did not work well this time; once the bridge started to tetter off to the side, we went. Obstacle three: walk your horse across a plastic tarp lying on the ground; we didn't get within 10 feet of the horse-eating plastic tarp. Next, follow a rolled-up tarp being dragged by another horse. It won't happen; it's time for me to get off! He was dancing and prancing so much that I had to get off (ok, not so bad if you know how to ride) and become an observer. The next task had the horse walk up to a tarp being held on each end so the horse could push the tarp with their chest; Terri came over and asked if she could give Amos a try at this obstacle. In short order, Terri had Amos push the tarp like a pro. The next challenge was to have the horse herd one of the trainers as you would in a crowd control maneuver. In 3 or 4 tries, he was working the person like a well-trained cutting horse; Terri said he was cutting off the person without giving him any cues once he realized what was expected. Terri then took Amos to the tarp on the ground, but not without some serious work, but accomplished it. Lastly, the rocking bridge, which she was not able to get him across, so I stepped in to lead him across, and since I was beside him, he never attempted to go off the side. It was a great learning experience for both of us; I watched Amos jump and prance around with someone else on him and discovered it was not all that bad. Amos learned that when I reach my limit, I get off! But I had set my goal, I would make it to the show ring and be an equestrian.

Chapter 10
Ready or Not: Here We Come Again!

Author's Note: Once again, Jim is back at the reins of the keyboard.

Jim

May finds Amos and Michelle going to their first showing experience, ready or not. This is an early season show, and being so early, many horses are not shed or clipped, but this is not held against the horse judged; it is the Wooly Show, the same show referred to in an earlier chapter. Michelle visited the entry booth and signed up for Walk/Trot, Western Riding, and Open classes. Terri and I were both in attendance to support her no matter the outcome and remind her she had not been riding all that long. Michelle was noticeably nervous and somewhat anxious about her first performance in the show ring with Amos. As Michelle rode in the class, Terri and I could see her nerves begin to show as we came closer to sending her into the arena. Of course, the rider controls the tone of the performance. Michelle answered the call into the arena with ten other entries, and as she rode Amos on the rail, Terri would coach her each time she passed our location. When the class was lined up, the results showed that Amos and Michelle placed 6th.

I know she was unsatisfied, but Terri and I were thrilled with her performance. She had only been riding for a few months, and Amos was still recovering from his ten years of exile. Showing horses has many facets; there are a significant number of things that need to come together all at once to provide results.

Michelle's second class was Western Riding; the arena was marked with various cones to indicate the starting and stopping locations of the requested gaits. The pattern called for a left lead at a certain point in the pattern. When Michelle performed the class, she inserted a right lead instead of the left lead. This was a significant mistake; Michelle received no awards in that class. When Michelle exited the arena, she was troubled and disappointed, not with Amos, but with her mistake of asking for the incorrect lead; true to form, Amos gave the rider precisely what the rider requested. Michelle was stressed and in pain, so she asked me to show Amos in class. I refused, so she requested Terri to show her the horse.

The last class Amos entered was the Western Pleasure Open, and Terri was thrilled to be back in the show ring with her old friend Amos. The class had only two entries, but instead of the lack of numbers, it was made up for in the quality of horsepower of the two entries. The judge worked the horses on the rail in their three gaits: walk, trot, and canter in both directions of the arena; once completed, he placed the horses on the rail for a second time and requested that the horses perform on the rail once again, and work both horses on the rail in both directions once again. Once the horses were lined up, the judge once again evaluated them and turned in his scorecard, and the announcer called the placing of the horses; first place and blue ribbon went to some number I do not recall, but the name was Diamond Amus, ridden by Terri Stutz. The ringmaster, also an Arabian judge, asked Terri if that was the same Amos that Jim Smith used to own. The response was yes, it is, and he does AGAIN. I can't say I was shocked by the results, but I know what Michelle's was. WOW! I could not believe it; 10 years and the people remembered this horse. All she could think was, now the pressure was on; she had to get better and fast. Everyone was watching this horse, judges, and competitors; they knew how great he was in the past and were wondering if, after all these years, he was still as good. I now knew Amos was, but I wasn't yet.

Michelle made plans to go to another show in June and asked me to show Amos since she would not be able to show him in all the classes; he was qualified to go in. It had been well over ten years since I performed in a show, so the day before the show, I knew I needed to brush up a bit. I planned to run him through a quick workout the day before the show. However, that is where the games began. I was about to put on a grand show for Michelle and had no idea it would happen. I asked for a trot on the rail and got a pace (Michelle said she had no idea he knew how to do that). Then, I asked for a left lead and got a right lead. I reversed on the rail, asked for a jog-trot, and again got pacing. At this point in my demonstration, Michelle laughs and shows no signs of stopping. I am on the rail, and I ask for the right lead. I get the left lead, convinced at this point that I have forgotten how to ride a horse, especially this one. I pulled Amos to the center of the arena to set him up as if waiting for the judge, and instead of standing squarely on all four feet, he parks like an American Saddlebred. Michelle is laughing her fool head off, and I am getting mad; I head for the rail to try again, and Amos decides it is the perfect time to demonstrate his ability to spin, nearly screwing himself into the ground.

Michelle was sure I had destroyed her showhorse and let me know. I yelled back at her. OK, you crawl on him and see if he does the same for you. Michelle climbs aboard, and Amos jogs as perfectly as any horse could. I was adamant about not performing the next day, but Michelle was not letting me off the hook; she was having too much fun at my total failure and Amos's sense of humor.

The following day at the show in the makeup ring, Amos was a bit silly, but the second they opened the gate for 15 horses to enter the arena, it was all business, and in the two classes we showed in, we placed second in each. Things were not so good for Michelle as we received more confirmation about how much Amos had been traumatized by the previous owners. Michelle had an excellent workout in the makeup arena, and when the gate was open for her class, she entered at a jog-trot as requested. Once all the horses entered the arena, the announcer informed the exhibitors that the horses were under the eye of the judge; Michelle was approximately ¾ of the way around the arena when the class officially started. As Amos and Michelle worked around to complete her first full lap in the arena, Amos suddenly began to lope and weave back and forth around the other horses in the arena like a car running the pylons; Michelle was yelling, "Coming Through, Coming Through." When Michelle got Amos back under control and stopped, she had done nearly a full lap in the arena. The ringmaster asked Michelle if she wanted to be excused from the arena, and she responded that she would like to finish the class. As expected, she did not place in the class of about 15 horses, and I was curious what went wrong. She told me that the previous owner was there and had called out over the rail, "Way to go, Michelle," he bolted a couple of steps later. I thought she was making an excuse; however, that was precisely what had transpired. My son was video recording her class, and he happened to be close to where the incident started; when the tape was played back, as clear as a bell, you could hear the former owner state those exact words, and two steps later, Amos was off to the races.

Michell continued to hone her equine skills, and progress was being made. She began to be quite competitive in the local Saturday Night shows. It was to the point that one horse, Harry, who was consistent in his performances, would typically be one place above her in the classes, and she won a lot of seconds behind Harry. Harry and his owner supported Michelle and Amos and regularly reported how well she was doing. Harry's owners even chatted in the arena while in the lineup waiting for the judge to place the class.

As supportive as Harry's family was, Michelle now had a goal; she was determined to place ahead of Harry.

Michelle's second year of showing Amos found me working many hours in my locomotive engineer career. The engineer I was training with was a big fan of horses, and we spoke a great deal about them. He also had a daughter who loved horses as much as her father, and in our discussions, we decided to allow his daughter Erin to show Amos in 4-H in halter classes. Erin spent many, many hours working with Amos in hand, and despite her efforts due to her physical disability, she just could not run fast enough to keep Amos at a trot, nor was she able to get and keep him squared up for the lineup and conformation (physical attributes of the breed standards) judging.

The day finally arrived for Amos and Erin to perform at the 4-H fair, and we were all there to help Erin perform well and provide a lot of moral support. Michelle and Erin put a great deal of time into getting Amos perfect in appearance for Erin's class. A couple of classes before Erin was going to compete, her father called her over to sit down in the chair next to him; as Erin moved to her chair, Amos walked over behind the chairs and hung his head between the two of them as if the 3 of them were having a football huddle. The discussion was to ensure Erin knew exactly what she would be required to do in the arena, as every halter class uses the same protocol. Once Erin confirmed to her father that she was confident in doing what she needed to do, we all walked to the makeup arena to prepare for Erin to exhibit Amos. When Erin was called into the arena, we watched as she took Amos into the arena and walked directly as her father instructed her; upon reaching the judge, standing approximately halfway down the arena, she was to begin trotting with Amos. As Erin started at her run, which was slow enough that Amos could walk and keep up, Amos started to trot, nearly in place but properly trotted down to the ringmaster, where she was required to stop and make a 90-degree turn with the horse towards the outer rail and walk over and stop and set the horse up and wait for the balance of the class to perform the exact routine. Erin's father walked down to the outside of the arena to view how Erin was doing; he reported that Amos was standing there perfectly, stating he could not have been a ¼ of an inch out of square and stood with all 4 feet planted firmly on the ground. Erin and Amos were recorded in 2nd place when the judge completed his class evaluation. Note that the horse that won the class was owned by a local veterinarian and had been exhibited at the Quarter Horse Congress, which is the largest Quarter Horse show in the United States. He had won the top 5 honors in his halter class. It appeared that Amos understood every word Erin's father had told them and performed each task without a single mistake. Not long after Erin's participation at the fair, her father invested in a nice horse for her to have and show in the future.

Michelle continued working hard, building her skills and confidence, and improving with every experience; they began operating as one. In late July, Michelle decided to go to a bigger show than she routinely attended. This was a Quarter Horse show, but they offered some classes for Arabian horses.

This show demonstrated all the hard work Michelle and Amos were putting in and were beginning to show results. The first class she entered was Arabian Western Pleasure, her first experience in a class A show, strictly with horses of the same breed. There were approximately 15 horses that answered the call into the arena, and when the class was complete and the smoke cleared, Michelle won her first major equine event. To say she was happy was an understatement; she was elated, and Terri and I were incredibly proud of her accomplishments. Michelle and Amos were next performing in a reining class, and compared to her first attempt at riding in a class in which she would be required to perform a pattern, the results showed her increased skill levels; in a rather large class, she scored a 4th place ranking. The 3rd and final class for the show was Open Western Pleasure, which again was a large class, and she retired from the arena for the day with 2nd place as well. She and Amos were becoming a formidable team.

Amos and Michelle set their sights on the Indiana Arabian Amateur show scheduled for August. The show turned out to be a rough spot for the progress that had been displayed in the previous show, but despite the disappointing results of the show, it confirmed what I had always told her about Amos: he did not make mistakes when it came to performing in a show ring. Although Michelle had such incredible success at the last show, the pressure of performing in an All-Arabian show and her hip causing her pain gave her doubts. The results were disheartening to Michelle that night, and we had a heated argument about them. Many mistakes in front of the judge caused her not to place well. The conversation that brought on the argument was a simple statement from Michelle that Amos took the improper lead in a class that Amos would have most likely won. Michelle was sitting in the grandstand watching another class after completing her entries. She was, no doubt, still fuming about my stating to her that Amos does not make mistakes in the show ring. As she reviewed her cues on the hard seat, she realized that due to her hip issues, she intended to give Amos one cue, but due to the hip issues, her weight more strongly asked him to take the opposite lead. She was bummed and kept saying poor Amos, having to deal with a poor rider. I can promise she never again had an issue like that, being the technician she was, and the problems of the horse and rider not communicating were solved. The one night of disaster created an incredible team that would have to be beaten. They worked as a team and kept getting better and better and BETTER!

The third season started well with regular rides in the winter, but since it was impossible to work out a location and time, lessons with Terri did not continue. Terri told Michelle to keep riding and practicing what she had been taught. Late in the spring, Michelle fell and broke her ankle, which required a walking cast, but with the walking cast, riding Amos was not working due to her lack of controlling the leg with the cast, and rather than cause problems, she made her Amos time a grooming and feeding treats exercise. Three days before the last show of the season in our area, her cast was removed, and having missed most of the show ring opportunities, she wanted to go to the show despite not having the chance to ride him for three months. On the day of the show, she spent extra time in the makeup arena before her class, and once the smoke had cleared, Michelle won the class. That was the moment it finally became clear; she now understood what I had been talking about with this horse. What a fantastic animal this Amos is. Year four finds us making plans for a significant life change, and we are not sure what this move has in store for us yet, especially when, Michelle decided to tune up Amos and go to a horse show. Another goal was about to be achieved; it was a local show, and Harry was in attendance. YEE HAA! We beat Harry, not just in one class, but in every class we were exhibiting together. She did not always win the class, but they placed above Harry in every class. She had set a significant goal for herself and Amos to boost her confidence further. It was time to ride off into the sunset with pride and confidence.

Chapter 11
Into the Sunset

Well, riding off into the sunset is not precisely what this was, but the sun does set in the west, and we were pulling up our stakes in Indiana and making a significant move to Wyoming. Why Wyoming, you ask? It is simply following our dreams. My Roy Rogers persona was rearing its ugly head once again. We had visited Wyoming two years earlier, and we both liked it. Things were well planned out when we packed up our belongings and began our cross-country move. Do I have any regrets? Only one. When I came home from work one day and announced to Michelle, "I am moving to Wyoming; you are welcome to come along if you like," it is the one thing I did not plan out well. We have spent 17 years in Wyoming. I am still reminded to this very day that she did not appreciate the vocabulary, and I would never live that down.

My research regarding moving a horse from the low elevation of Indiana to a mountain state like Wyoming enlightened me that it can present serious problems for livestock, with elevation sickness being the most prominent issue; some animals do not adjust. Amos was significant to us, and Michelle and I held him in the highest regard. We planned to take Amos out west with us, but just in case, we needed to have a backup plan. That backup plan was Terri. We asked her if we got to Wyoming and Amos did not adjust properly, would she take him for the balance of his life. I would not sell him as I had once before; I would not make that mistake again. Knowing Terri's love and respect for Amos, I knew that was the ONLY option available. Terri agreed that if there were a problem, she would take care of him, and I knew he would be loved and well cared for. So, the horse's move was the final loaded trip from Indiana, along with three dogs and a cockatiel.

Upon our arrival at our new home in Wyoming, Amos was placed in a small pasture with a flowing stream for water and grass for grazing. Wyoming was a culture shock for us all. I had rented a house on a working cattle ranch of about 26,000 acres in northeast Wyoming near Gillette. Horses are not kept in stalls at almost every ranch, not in the summer, winter, rain, hail, or snow. When we talked with the landlord about our concerns about not having some shelter for our horse, he offered to pay for the supplies needed for a shed if Michelle and I were willing to build it. Before long, Amos had a 3-sided shed for protection, and we both were pleased to have him protected. We quickly learned that our idea of riding differed from a ride on the ranch; you could ride for hours on end, never see another soul, and get as rugged as one may want. We discovered we needed another horse to ride together, so the search for a second horse and a pasture mate began in earnest.

We attended a horse sale, bought a Missouri Fox Trotter mare, and hauled her home. The following day, we discovered that the landlord did not allow mares on the ranch, so we found someone willing to trade a 5-year-old wild Mustang gelding even up for the mare. We now had a Mustang for riding together rather than the tag team approach. At age 4, the Mustang had been captured in the southwest of Wyoming and had gone through the renowned Honor Farm Wild Horse Training Program, which had turned Big into a nice riding horse. Big's name came from being huge, standing 15.2 hands, and significantly more significant than the typical wild Mustang. Being captured at the age of four gave Big considerable experience in the wild, which made them an excellent horse in the mountains and provided some enlightening experiences there. Amos and Big were good friends and complimented each other on our mountain adventures.

Our first major trip to the mountains with Amos and Big started as usual, with the arrival at the trailhead, parking of the rig, and tacking up the horses for a ride. The trailhead parking lot was abandoned, as only two other rigs existed. We headed on the trail to explore this new location and all its wonders. He was traveling down the trail, gaining elevation as we rode. Rounding a curve in the trail, we broke into a large clearing surrounded by ridges to the bellowing of a brood cow calling for her calf. Momma was up on the ridge side a couple of hundred yards up when suddenly we heard the calf call back to its mother but could not see it. But moments later, the calf came busting out of the brush about fifty yards away, heading towards a figure in the clearing that it assumed to be its mother. At this point, the very near-sighted calf was running to what it believed was its mother, and Amos was the object of its affection. Seconds later, Amos thought he was being attacked by a strange wild animal and, in true fashion, saved the rider and himself. He was trying to bolt in the opposite direction with a spin; Michelle was frantically attempting to get him stopped, under control, and facing his attacker, and Michelle accomplished it. The fantastic part of this is that it all took place in the amount of time that Mr. Magoo of the bovine world got within 25 feet of Amos while traveling at an aggressive lope to close the gap, meaning very quickly. Once the calf realized Amos was not its mother, it turned, heading up the mountain to its bellowing mother. Amos might have covered five strides before Michelle had him back under control, still centered astride him. Being upset by the ordeal that had just occurred, she turned and saw her husband busting a gut laughing at the rodeo he had just witnessed. I told her how proud I was of how she managed the situation and regained control quickly; I told her that having ridden that situation out and staying on top of Amos, she had become a rider, not just a horsesitter. The balance of the ride was relatively leisurely and extremely enjoyable.

The mountains kept calling Michelle and me, and we spent many hours riding in this fantastic country. The hills might be home to Big, but they sometimes presented a challenge to Amos. One of the most significant issues was crossing mountain streams. Big was always ridden across first since he had no issue with the streams; he had a habit of sticking his nostrils down into the water and blowing, making the water explode around his head and making a loud noise. This had convinced Amos that the Lock Ness monster resided in the mountain streams of Wyoming. After many failed attempts to allow Big to lead the way without terrorizing Amos, the next trip across a stream Amos WOULD be crossing first. Being in the mountains, it did not take long to find the next stream, and as planned, I had Michelle attempt the stream crossing. It is not that once could not get him to cross; it was never a smooth transition; he resisted and forced the rider to be stern and not accept a refusal. A 15-minute battle of the minds resulted in Amos facing back on the other side of the stream, watching Big and I wading into the stream. True to form, Big drops his nose into the stream and blows bubbles, spraying water in every direction. Then, he takes a drink and passes across. On the return trip to the trailer, stream crossings were remarkedly smoother following the new stream crossing protocol. Amos surprisingly understood that Big was causing the issue, not a monster in the stream. Along with Amos's ability to learn quickly and figure things out independently, watching Big was no exception.

Amos turned into a perfect mountain trail horse; although Amos had been ridden several times on back roads for exercise, he was a show horse, and this type of riding was foreign to him. Big was of significant help in giving confidence to Amos as we faced the

HORRORS of the Wild West backcountry. Amos quickly became a solid mountain trail horse, adjusting to the much less stressful riding he had not always been in. In the show tack, he would puff himself up, presenting himself in a much bolder appearance than in the mountains. On the mountain rides, humans needed to adjust to be like rustic early settlers without having bathrooms and outhouses. Michelle and I were raised in rural areas, not always in modern situations, so it did not create a problem for us. Since we often had friends riding with us, we adopted a respectful honor system when the urge appeared. We would announce we needed to make a pit stop, the rider in need would pull off the side of the trail where there was a safe and protected area, and the riders' balance would position themselves facing away to provide privacy. The policy worked well for all involved as we spent many days in the mountains enjoying their majesty and beauty up close. On one trip, Michelle and I were riding in the mountains, and she started remarking on how relaxed Amos had become riding in the mountains. We stopped on the trail to swap horses so I could experience this laid-back Amos and again started down the trail. It was a different ride, with Amos going down the trail on loose, sloppy rein and making no contact with the bit. As we had a leisurely ride down the mountain, I gave Amos his head, and he followed the trail. I remarked to Michelle how different it was to experience this attitude. Just as I noted the situation, Amos began veering off the trail. I told Michelle I did not know what he was doing but that I should let him go and see what happened. Amos walked about twenty feet off the trail to a semi-open area, stopped, assumed the position, relieved his bladder, made a direct path back to the trail, and proceeded. This was one of those times when Amos's actions of Amos boggled my mind. Sometimes, he acts like he has a human mind, and his response is as unique as it is humorous. I never understood Amos's thinking process, but I knew he was our exceptional Amos, even out of the show ring, and he continued to bless our lives.

He was in the Wild West on a ranch, exposing Amos to various wildlife and hunting with the scent of wild animals, alive and dead. I have witnessed very spectacular reactions by horses getting a nose full of a strange new aroma. When hunting season began, there was a continuous rotation of out-of-state hunters staying and hunting on the ranch. This was a terrific opportunity to introduce Amos to a new experience, a visit to the meat shed, which was part of the program. On the way to the meat shed, we ran into Bill, the ranch owner, and he told Michelle to be careful as there was wild game in the shed, and he did not want her to get hurt by her panicking horse. We went to the meat shed and readied ourselves for a reaction. Michelle dismounted, approached the shed, and began encouraging Amos to move inside to investigate the carcass. Amos walked directly into the door without hesitation, continued up to the carcass, sniffed it intently, turned, and quietly walked out the doorway to say, so what a dead Pronghorn. Now, when are we going to go riding? I was expecting a negative response, and true to form, Amos already had a handle on it. His love for life, the show ring, mountain riding, and the nightly running of roping steers in the arena since roping was an essential activity to the ranch owner. Amos enjoyed herding the steers to the opposite end of the arena after the roper completed their run and readied themselves to go again. Along with the trail riding and turning the roping steers into their pen, Amos wanted more excitement, so he created a pasture game. For most who experienced the game, it was not necessarily well received unless you knew Amos well. Upon entry to the pasture, Amos would bolt directly at you and come to a screeching halt a few feet away or do a flyby mere inches away. I am aware of the danger that situation could be, but there was not even a close call in all the years he played that game. I am thankful for that, but I never felt threatened by his actions; I honestly had the ultimate trust in him.

I can honestly say without a doubt that the years in Wyoming up to now have been incredible; what an experience of riding horses on a ranch, moving cattle, riding a horse in the mountains in remote, pristine areas, imagining this is what the early settlers saw, and it is still genuinely awe-inspiring. Michelle loved riding in the hills but much preferred not excessively rough riding, and for sure, with the cattle, they would push but not want the speed required for a runaway. As much as she enjoyed our current lifestyle of horse camping in the mountains, she craved the show ring, a place she felt comfortable in, which added to her competitive side and required that I begin looking. She had shared a situation that had occurred at work regarding a co-worker. This co-worker seemed to think that losing a considerable amount of financial settlement money in the horse industry would make him an expert in everything equine, and Michelle took exception to it. The remark made to Michelle after seeing a photo of herself sitting on Amos was that he was a nice horse, but he dropped his shoulder when loping. Even Michelle was equine smart enough to realize one cannot determine if a horse drops its shoulder while loping if you have never seen the horse loping. Michelle knew what a machine Amos was in the show ring and wanted to prove to this fellow that Amos was an incredible athlete. I was given my marching order, and the search for a horse show began.

Chapter 12
Return to the Show Ring

I had received my orders loud and clear and was tasked with finding a horse show for Michelle and Amos. I may have had my fill of the showering competition, but that was not so with Michelle. She has been highly competitive since I have known her and showed no signs of throwing in the towel. I started looking for shows that offered Western Pleasure Classes, like the small Saturday night shows she enjoyed back in Indiana. But this was Wyoming, and their idea of a horse show was a rodeo, and I knew barrel racing or goat tying would not be Michelle's idea of a good time. My best efforts seemed to come up short on the horse search. So, I thought if I got on the website of the Arabian Horse Association, maybe I could find a show that would fit the bill. With the odds against me, I found a show in Billings, Montana, a four-hour drive away.

The show in Montana was not a Saturday night show; this was a Class A qualifying show for the Region 6 Regional Championship. Having found a show, we needed to put a plan together to get her there.

We had a truck and a horse trailer, the wife already had riding clothes, and the show was scheduled for our off days. This looks doable as Michelle has been riding for several years, and she and Amos have developed into a respectable team. The missing link at this point is tuning Amos up to show status, and Terri, our trainer, was over 1000 miles east. I am unsure how to resolve the issue; the best we can do is call Terri. The call to Terri was put out, and a message was left on her phone; within a couple of days, we had a response. Terri, having initially trained Amos and done the same for Michelle, made her believe it would not be a problem; she could guide Michelle on bringing Amos back to show ring status. The work was about to begin earnestly to get Michelle and Amos back to the show ring. Michelle started with planning with Terry on how, what, and when to work to get on the road back to competition. Michelle worked tirelessly in the roping arena with Amos; when I was available, I was the ground man, critic, and part-time camera operator to review the progress. The roping arena was in front of the main house that belonged to the landlord, Bill, and it did not go unnoticed that Michelle was putting in hours of serious work to get Amos ready for a show. From the minute we arrived at the ranch, the joke from Bill was that Amos was a "Sissy Show Horse," which was never taken as an insult, knowing Bill was a rancher and roper and had never been around a western pleasure horse. Between the phone calls to Terri, the hours of saddle time riding Amos, the effort I put in, and shoeing by our blacksmith, Amos again looked to be in serious show-horse mode. I had all the faith in the world in his ability and knew Terri knew what she was doing, and no doubt Michelle was not afraid of putting in demanding work, and the results were beginning to show. One of the early requirements was for Michelle to update her Amateur Card to allow her to complete it in Billings. With all the "I's" dotted and the "T's" crossed, we were heading to Billings. After three months of consistent work behind her, Michelle felt pleased with Amos and her accomplishments and excited to show Amos again.

Upon our arrival at the Billing Horse Complex, we registered and confirmed the entries for Amos and Michelle and put Amos in the stall to relax a bit from his long trailer ride. We quickly met the neighboring horse owners in adjoining stalls and noticed a young lady crying and sad in front of a stall. Upon talking with her, she shared with us that on the trip to the show grounds, her horse had been injured and would not be able to compete due to the severity of the injury, which made us very sad for her as well. Shortly after discovering the young lady's situation, Michelle and I decided that if her parents would allow her, and she got along okay with Amos and could make him work, we would allow her to show Amos in the Juvenile class. Within minutes, she was smiling again and helping get Amos tacked up and out into the practice arena for a first ride. As expected, the young lady was a good rider and quickly learned to cue Amos. The next day, we would do another practice with the young lady and Michelle to prepare for the afternoon classes. As the class time neared for the young lady, I became her groom as Michelle would be competing in a class a few classes after the Juvenile Division class. Amos and his young rider appeared from the class with no ribbon but had a huge smile. She got the opportunity to ride; Michelle then competed in the Amateur Division, emerging with a second-place ribbon. All were seen as outstanding results for the day, and Michelle had one more class to perform the following day. We arrived bright and early the following day to prepare for the Open Western Pleasure class. The Open divisions are the only classes where professional trainers can compete; however, amateur riders can show in them. This class would be challenging, being the best of the best in attendance at the show. Preparations for the class went well, with practice arena work, after-work roll, bathing, and general show grooming completed. Michelle headed into the area with thirteen other Western pleasure horses to answer the call. Michelle made a great ride, and when the ribbons were awarded, Michelle and Amos retired with a first-place ranking. Michelle and Amos both had reaped the rewards of hard, dedicated work. Michelle had entered the realm of being a ligament contender in Wester Pleasure with her performance. Saying I was very proud of Michelle and Amos would be a colossal understatement.

The results of Billings were terrific and set the stage for another horse show that we had not even considered. A qualifying show in the top two allows for entry into the Regional Championships; now, Amos has qualified in Amateur and Open Western Pleasure. Michelle and I were thrilled at the results. About a week after the Billings show, one of the young ladies that we had met in Billings contacted us to see if she could ride Amos in another show to attempt to qualify him in the Juvenile Division; Michelle agreed and decided to transport Amos to a show in Douglas Wyoming and allow the young lady to show him. The results indicated a qualification in the juvenile division as well. All efforts were now being focused on the International Arabian Horse Association Region 6 Championships, to be held in Gillette, Wyoming, a mere twenty miles from where we resided. Michelle was now qualified to compete; it was not of conscious intent, just the results of her going to an available horse show; now Michelle and Amos were in a fantastic position; this was a chance to qualify for the big dance, the U.S. Arabian Nationals.

The summer at the ranch was spent on continued work to attend the Regionals in Gillette, Wyoming. As Michelle was busy preparing Amos for the Regionals, our horseshoer asked us about his daughter and the need for a reining horse for her 4-H Queen competition. She was in high school and a 4-H member and had been selected to contend for the Wyoming State 4-H Queen competition. Bob, our horseshoer, and father of Amanda, asked if we would consider allowing Amanda to use Amos in the State Fair competition. Bob tried to tell Amanda about Amos, but Amanda responded 100% Wyoming Barrel Racing Cowgirl, "I am not riding an Arab." I was not surprised by the response; I have heard many refer to Arabians as being crazy horses. However, I have also witnessed Amos changing those attitudes countless times when doubters met him. Understand that Amanda had never ridden an Arabian, nor had she ever seen Amos, and all she knew was barrel racing horses, which were Quarter horses. Bob had a tough time convincing Amanda to come over and see Amos and try him out. Knowing she would give him a chance, Michelle went into tune-up mode with Amos on another discipline, reigning. Amos was well versed in reigning other than performing a rollback, as Michelle did not desire to have that in her bag of tricks. Amos could perform flying lead changes in one step every time the command was given, and riding circles at varied speeds were also efficiently carried out. Performing a rollback requires a horse to run down the length of the arena, coming to a quick but controlled stop, immediately spinning on its haunches, and immediately resume a run on the exact path to the opposite end of the arena, was accomplished in a couple of days riding due to the excellent handling and athletic ability of the Amos. The night of Amanda's introduction to Amos arrived, and we were informed after the first try that Amanda made it known to her mother that she would not like Amos during the entire drive to our location. But apparently, driving up the long lane to the ranch and seeing the stunning looks of Amos in the arena with Michelle was a mind-altering experience. Amanda immediately fell in love with the beauty of Amos and his ability, and their performance at The Wyoming State Fair was put on the schedule.

A week before Regionals, Amos got extremely sick and had to be rushed to the local veterinary clinic due to severe colic (equine bellyache). Michelle was at the ranch alone and unable to tow our trailer because the ball hitch was in my truck, and I was at work, so she called and asked the ranch owner if she could use his truck and trailer to haul Amos to the vet clinic. Of course, Bill said yes, so Michelle pulled the rig, a full-sized dual-wheeled pickup with a full eight-foot bed attached to a 30-foot gooseneck trailer. Michelle pulled the rig down toward the pasture and turned it to go out the back entrance, as she could not back this big of a rig. She worked at getting Amos to his feet since he was down and did not want to stand. Once on his feet, she gets Amos shagged into the trailer and gets ready to head out the back drive and around the house to get to the vet clinic as quickly as possible. As she continued the drive, she had to pass a suburban used by the visiting hunters, who had left the door open. She proceeded to tear the door entirely off the suburban, which she did not know about until the following morning. She drives twenty miles to town and pulls into the parking lot of the vet clinic, where she removes the back bumper of the vet's brand-new pickup truck. Amos was kept overnight at the clinic, where he was administered 25 liters of fluid due to his severe dehydration. It was a costly vet visit, and the most expensive part was NOT what they did to treat Amos. Thankfully, Amos survived the colic, but the veterinarian informed Michelle that due to the severity and trauma he had endured, Amos would not recover sufficiently to compete in the upcoming show. We were grateful for the vet saving Amos' life and respected what they recommended regarding pushing him and causing him stress. Amazingly, Amos bounced all over the pasture two days later like nothing had happened. On the third day and after much discussion, the decision was made to give him a light workout to take the rough edge off his anxiety, hopefully. The following day, he was more anxious in the pasture and showed no signs of distress from working the previous day. We allowed Amos to dictate what he was capable of and watched how he responded to the work so as not to over-stress him. As we monitored Amos and saw no ill effects, we decided to continue our plans to show Amos at the regionals. The decision was not taken lightly, as he had been seriously ill, but we also knew him well enough to understand his response.

The day finally arrived, and they headed into Gillette to make their entries and register Amos to compete. When Michelle came to enter the class, the show secretary began to question the name of the trainer she was riding under. Michelle replied that she did not have a trainer on-site, and the show secretary told her that she would not be able to exhibit without a trainer. Michelle had studied the Arabian Horse Association rule book and knew it was unnecessary. Although it is normal for riders to go to the shows under the tutelage of a professional trainer, it is not a requirement. Michelle calmly asked the secretary to point that rule out, pointing to the rule book on the entry table. The secretary said it was not required but strongly suggested, and at that, she allowed Michelle to complete the entry and registration. Michelle headed to the stalls assigned to her and readied them to put Amos in and let him relax. Amos would spend the balance of the day and the night at the regional showgrounds. The next morning, Michelle would be loading Amos back into the trailer and hauling him 2 hours south to Douglas, Wyoming, home of the Wyoming State Fair. The entire day would be spent with Amanda competing in the 4-H Fair Queen competition; Amanda placed third in her contest. Michelle spent the night sleeping in her truck, leaving early the following day to return to the regional completion. Returning to the regional arena, she rode Amos to prepare for her classes. The young lady who had qualified Amos in the juvenile division showed him Saturday morning but failed to qualify him for nationals. Michelle competed in two classes on Saturday night but could not qualify in the first, and the other took second place. Sunday morning, Amos and one of the juvenile riders had a class and qualified for U.S Arabian Nationals in the juvenile rider division. Six classes of completion in 4 days, traveling 300 miles between the State Fair competition and the regional performances, resulting in qualifying in two divisions for the U.S. Nationals and placing 3rd in the Wyoming 4-H Queen competition, all of that shortly after being treated for colic and dehydration, receiving 25 liters of fluid overnight at the vet clinic, on top of all of that, Amos is 21 years old when accomplishing all of it, no doubt an AMAZING horse.

The decision not to attend the U.S. Nationals was made due to the extreme expense of attending and competing in such a high-level competition, which was simply something that we could not afford to do. Shortly after the Regional Championships, we received a postcard in the mail. It was from the International Arabian Horse Association (IAHA), stating congratulations. I smiled at it and then tossed it in the trash since it did not appear significant. A couple of months later, we again received a second postcard regarding Amos; this postcard stated something about having his points tallied. For more information, call the number listed to inquire. I called the number listed, and the voice on the other end announced I had contacted the IAHA headquarters. When I inquired about receiving the postcard, they asked a few questions to confirm my identity and that we indeed own the horse. Upon confirming the information, they continued stating it was regarding an award he had won. Unknown to either of us, Michelle, while applying for an amateur card, had inadvertently entered Amos in the awards program for Arabian Western Pleasure horses to earn points in the Horse of the Year competition. We were surprised to hear this and even more surprised when they informed us Diamond Amus (Amos) had won Horse of the Year honors in Region 6. Region 6 covers horses exhibited in IAHA-sanctioned shows in Montana, Wyoming, North Dakota, and South Dakota. Not only did he win Western Pleasure Horse of the Year honors, but all three divisions, Juvenile, Amateur, and Open, would also be awarded a vest for each division he won. They requested a photo of Amos with the rights to publish it in their Annual Awards edition magazine, glossy pages, and all. We obtained permission to make copies of his award photo at the regionals and sent it to the IAHA. A few weeks later, a package arrived with three award vests with his name and accomplishment embroidered for Amos' achievements. Michelle and I each had a vest, and it was no doubt where the third one belonged; Terri, our trainer, was thrilled and honored to be included in the award. After all the years, I am still blown away by what this horse continues to accomplish: Horse of the Year in Western Pleasure, Amos had retired all three divisions in 3 shows. That speaks volumes about Amos's talent and skill and Michelle's hard work.

Michelle's accomplishments proved to all, especially those who doubted him being a legitimate showhorse. Moreover, Amos proved to Michelle that he was as incredible as we always told her. Michelle now feels the love and admiration for what Amos allowed her to accomplish; she didn't start riding until the age of 45 and worked and pushed herself to learn how to ride and had to overcome a lot of her fears, adding another obstacle was the fact she had an artificial hip as well and all on top of the issues created by the poor treatment by the interim owners.

Chapter 13
Git Along Little Dogie

We were beginning a new phase in our life with Amos since the decision to retire from the Western Pleasure showing. However, in no way, shape, or form means that Amos would spend the balance of his life eating grass and treats. As is the typical case with Arabian horses, they need constant mental stimulation as they get mentally and emotionally bored. The training process for Arabians versus Quarter Horses is different; the method that works well on a Quarter Horse does not work the best on an Arabian. As an owner and trainer, one must discern what is necessary to obtain the best results no matter what breed a person is working with; just like people, each animal is different, and what works on one may or may not work on the next. As much as Amos enjoyed eating grass and getting treats, I knew that lifestyle would not satisfy his desire to be active and mentally stimulated.

Throughout most of Michelle's shows and conditioning career, I was the ground man, assisting in getting the finer details to the rider's attention. I spent very little time riding Amos, as the goal was to help Michelle and Amos bond and become successful. With the exit from the show ring, I was going to be able to spend time in the saddle with Amos. I was going to revert to my childhood dream of being a cowboy, as Amos was already past being traumatized by cattle. I thought it would be fun to let Amos show his athletic ability and begin working cattle. We already knew he loved the fast-moving pace it could provide, and Michelle wanted no part of that type of riding. I set my goal of riding in the local fair in the Working Cow Horse competition.

This performance of Arabians was not unheard of as the U.S. Nationals had classes, and Arabians were quite good at performing these tasks. The horse and rider must take a single steer and work it back and forth across the end of an arena between two flags posted on the rail. Following that, the rider is expected to work the steer down the side of the arena at a relatively quick speed, forcing the steer to reverse direction several times; once that is completed, the rider is required to push the steer into the center of the arena and circle the steer in both directions, all of these actions were to be completed within a 3-minute window. The goal is for the horse and rider team to direct the steer into performing the expected moves quickly and orderly, demonstrating the team's ability to control the steer. I had this entire first session worked out in my head, knowing I could have total control of Amos to position him exactly where he needed to go. I had access to a pen of roping steers, and having worked them in the arena after the roper's hand caught them and released them, I had a good sense of which steer would be cooperative.

I pulled Amos from his pasture and tacked him up in his reigning equipment to protect him as we attempted to work cattle. True to form, once the specific equipment was applied, Amos adopted the mindset that the equipment required. This would be a low-key introduction to lay the groundwork for grooming him into my lifelong dream of having a cowhorse. Once Amos and I arrived at the arena, I tied him to the rail as I brought my chosen steer into the arena; I mounted Amos and began quietly riding alongside the steer wherever the calf moved. Amos followed the calf as I directed him; the calf going easy along the rail allowed me to direct him at my will. Fifteen minutes into the ride, we began to increase the speed of our ride, and things continued to progress as I expected. Amos followed cattle like a duck takes to water. I decided to attempt to maneuver my steer back and forth between the flags at the end of the arena, which required a minimum of three changes of direction between the flags. The calf was handled exactly as I had hoped, and Amos was spot-on in responding to my requests. The next step was to push the steer down the length of the arena, turning the calf a minimum of 3 times on the rail, being a longer stretch to work the calf on and at a faster speed. In the rail work, I discovered an issue; as I pushed the calf, Amos did not understand I needed him to pass the calf and cut it off, forcing a reversal. My continued squeezing on his sides was not getting the pass to happen. As we neared the end of the arena, I touched him with a spur to complete the pass and reigned him across in front of the calf. Once I finished my first turn, I was already planning what I needed to complete the move again. The calf was already moving quickly down the rail, and I needed to get there fast as the calf was already halfway down the length of the arena. I needed to complete the turn before the calf reached the end of the arena. I reined Amos to the left and touched him with a spur to catch up and pass the calf to execute a turn ahead of the calf and complete the second turn on the rail. Amos was also considering the next move, and immediately as I touched him with the spur and turned him to the left, he launched toward the calf at HIGH speed. He closed the gap in seconds, passed the calf, and dived in front of the calf. I was not expecting such an abrupt maneuver to occur and came dangerously close to not staying seated on Amos during this move. Once again, Amos demonstrated his ability to immediately pick up on what we were doing.

Amos and I continued to work on our cattle working skills, but unfortunately, a week before the competition, Amos suffered an injury to his front leg, and I was forced to stop the training and allow him to heal. We could begin riding him again several weeks later, but the fair was over, and we did not get to compete. Although we did not get to complete at the fair, we did our fair share of working cattle on the ranch. Ranch work does not involve a pattern or a time limit; it is just a simple plan: get said cattle from point A to point B as safely and efficiently as possible. Most often, it was gathering cattle from one large pasture and driving them to another when grazing was sparse. These were mostly steady, slow moves as the cows had calves at their sides and generally knew what was happening when the move started, but not so much with the calves as they were free spirits and did not care where we wanted them to go.

One unique cattle venture occurred when the neighboring ranch had a group of 2-year-old heifers get out of their pasture, and we needed to get them sorted out from the ranch cattle. Michelle was trying to assist in the move, and Bill, the ranch owner, was hauling our horses but could not ride as he had recently had shoulder surgery. The invading heifers were not interested in being herded in any reasonable manner. It was a cold and rainy day, which seemed to encourage the heifers to be even more cantankerous. From the start of the operation, it was far and above what Michelle felt comfortable doing, so she loaded her horse into the trailer and sat in the truck with Bill. These heifers were what we called rangy, which means WILD; they wanted nothing to do with human intervention in their world. The area we were trying to perform this work on was hilly and covered in 2-foot-high sagebrush, and nothing about this project was slow and easy; this was wild, high-speed action, and I was having the time of my life, and Amos did a fantastic job. I was unaware of the fact, but Bill and Michelle sat in the truck the entire time, hooting and hollering, cheering me on. Bill said to Michelle, "That little Arab can work cows," which was one of the greatest compliments we could receive, especially since a true cowboy gave it. Bill acknowledged with his statement that his view of Arabians had changed.

Michelle would accompany cattle moves regularly, and her position was to follow the herd as a pusher, allow the rest of us to gather and put the wayward cattle back into the herd when they tried to break away. One memorable cattle gathering occurred in spring while the brood cows were calving. The herd needed to be moved due to the lack of quality pasture for the lactating cows to nourish their new calves. We rode in a pasture with many ravines for the cattle to hide in; the terrain was extremely rugged. We had broken up into teams of 2-3 riders trying to cover the pasture in an orderly fashion. Michelle was stationed in a location to hold the cattle close to the gate. Once we gathered the small groups, we returned them to the gathering point for Michelle to hold. I was working a small ravine and came across 5 or 6 head of cows with calves and was turning them toward the gathering point for Michelle. The landlord's wife was riding near me and came to assist in moving the group. As we slowly drove the group to the gate area, we saw a horse and rider running hard, leaving a trail of dust in their wake. Although we were pretty far from the rider, we could tell by the outfit it was Michelle. Cindy remarked, "I have to go save Michelle," and took off like a rocket across the pasture as hard as she could. When I got to the gathering point, quite a herd was gathered by then.

In the distance, I could see Cindy and Michelle coming to the gathering point but saw no cattle. Once Michelle arrived, she described how one of the cows she had in the holding area decided to run to the hills, and Amos decided it was his place not to allow the rascal to get away. Michelle said she did get to the runaway cow, but as hard as she tried, she could not get the cow turned back to join the herd. Michelle was no worse for wear but made it clear that from then on was only going to be a pusher. Two days later, the runaway cow with a tiny new calf was at the pasture gate, ready to join the rest of the herd.

After retiring Amos from the show ring, we are experiencing many enjoyable hours of riding, whether gathering cattle for sorting or branding, relaxing rides in the mountains enjoying God's handwork, or simply turning back cattle in the roping arena for the competition ropers. Amos always gave his best and spread joy for two of his greatest fans and his biggest admirers.

Chapter 14
A Diamond Never Loses Its Shine

Since we officially retired Amos from the competitions, he has never ceased inspiring us with his talent, love of working, and desire to find new ways to keep us smiling. Amos became my hunting horse and was never required to be a pack animal. We felt he deserved special treatment at 21, winning horse of the year honors and qualifying for the Arabian U.S. Nationals. He would gladly tote me up the mountain and be beside me on many elk hunts. We were still working the seven days on seven days off schedule and had plenty of time to go to the mountains, enjoy the beauty of God's creation, and view all of its wonders. We often explored new areas and found new wonders; it was a never-ending search.

Whether it was moving a herd of cattle to a new pasture, gathering cows and calves for brandings, a pleasure ride in the mountain, or hunting an elusive elk, he supplied the courage, confidence, and power to get the job done. Many times, riding in the mountains or in the remote locations of the ranch, we assisted in a project; it seemed mostly a time for self-evaluation and soul-searching, much like this writing project has turned out to be for me. Sitting and reliving many of the events between Amos and me had been fulfilling, heartwarming, and incredible to watch but also thrilling to be a part of. Do I have regrets? Yes, without a doubt. If I had been able to do things differently at the time, I would have done that. I can honestly admit I only have a few things I wish had happened that would have made my relationship more perfect than I believe it already was. First, I could not financially promote Amos to share him with more people in the horse industry. Second, as hard as I tried, I could never make contact with Mr. Wayne Newton. I have never been one that felt like my life would not be complete without fame and fortune. My desire to connect with Mr. Wayne Newton was to personally thank him for being a horse lover, as well as to share how his contribution to the Arabian Horse world had spanned the industry as well and for allowing simple folks like me to share in what I feel was one of the most incredible experiences in my horse career, to have shared the wonders of Amos. Lastly, I wish there had been more mares bred to allow Amos a lasting legacy of his superior attributes that made him an incredible athlete, show horse, and dear friend to our family.

Just being on Amos provided the rider with confidence and pride. I can't say enough about my pride in ownership and admiration for Amos and what he has provided for our lives. It has been the highest honor to have had him as a member of our family; he was far more than just a prized possession; he was a friend and companion who allowed me to be a part of his extraordinary life. He touched many lives, directly and indirectly, in many different ways. To me, Amos was every bit as great as Roy Rogers' Trigger, Gene Autry's Champion, and Penny Tweedy's Secretariat; Amos was all of these to me.

As with many things, time can be our enemy or our friend. Time causes us to rush, not even noticing the amazing things happening right before our eyes. Everyone experiences stress; the pressures of life are incredibly high these days, and demanding work schedules, along with family issues and responsibilities can quickly take one to their limits; the world is much smaller these days and, I believe, much crazier. Amos could get you back in the rough canyons or high in the mountains, help you forget your problems, and be grateful for visiting those rough areas. I am always amazed when spending time on a horse in the mountains and how the little things have caught my eye. The mountain flowers, the shapes of trees and rocks, the fungi that grow in darker, wetter areas. Astounding colors and textures, shapes, and even specific locations thrill the soul. I try my best to allow my inner child to guide my vision of the world from where I am. Honestly, it was a humbling and awe-inspiring experience. Each of us is affected by our environment; our bodies and minds, heat, and cold weather conditions all mold our attitudes and moods. One's outlook on life affects how smooth everyday life will be. I have discovered through the writing of this book that my attitude towards life has changed me. I was angry with how our world was all about me, myself, and I, and how others do not matter provided we as individuals get what we want—working in corporate America with disregard for its employees. Through all his memories, Amos has helped me realize I have had a fantastic life in the equine industry I had chosen. I now go to work with a grin and realize that my peace and joy cannot be taken from me. Thank you, Amos, for bringing joy to me one more time. As heat and pressure affect our lives, it also creates one of nature's most valuable and beautiful wonders, the diamond. Amos was my living diamond, the countless hours of effort he put into perfecting his gaits at the guidance of the trainers. The pressure of competition at the highest levels he was exposed to, as well as his work ethic and desire to please. From a natural, uncut, rugged gemstone rough around the edges into the stunning multi-faceted shimmering gem he became.

We were on our way to work three years following his regional championship. I answered the phone, and it was the ranch owner. He said he hated to tell me, but we found your Arabian dead in the pasture a little while ago. The news took me aback, as we were on the mountain elk hunting less than a week earlier. What was worse was the fact I had to tell Michelle. He informed me that he would take care of him so that Michelle did not have to deal with that experience when we got home. I knew he was taking this action as not too long before I was asked to assist in the loss of one of his favorite horses that he dearly loved, and he was returning the favor, as he, too, admired Amos. Upon returning home from work, we talked with Bill, wanting to know the details of his death. Bill proceeded to describe the situation, which was confirmed by his wife as well; he had reached into the hay feeder, got a mouth full of hay, removed his head, and fell to the ground with the hay still sticking out of his mouth. He assured us that his death appeared to be sudden with no suffering as there was not the first scuff mark on the ground from thrashing his legs. As difficult as it was to know we lost our beloved Amos, we were relieved to hear that he did not suffer.

My greatest hope is that this book depicts the love and admiration I have for the time I was able to spend with this incredible creature of God's creation. Michelle and I consider ourselves extremely blessed to have had the privilege to have such a unique animal in our lives. He provided so much joy and pride in serving us and doing his best, which always impressed us as owners. All the stories were factual, and I hope they touch your heart as much as he touched ours. My last ride on Amos was to Elk Camp, which was as thrilling as my first. We were hunting in a new area, so we were both learning it. We came across some very soft ground as we followed a long-sloping clearing. Trying to be cautious to avoid any problems, Amos' right front foot suddenly sank deep into the ground about halfway to his knee. He instantly reared on his back legs, pivoted 180 degrees, and launched with his back legs; we touched back down about 6 feet from where we had been and are now standing on solid footing in seconds. As violent as the maneuver may sound in this writing, it was amazingly smoothly performed and precisely executed to get us both to safety. I understand that may have been an aggressive move, but being a seasoned rider and constantly trying to stay centered on my mount, I found it to be an amazingly smooth and quick response rather than a panicked one. Once again, his power, athletic ability, and care for his rider made a safe trip home.

It has been many years now since we lost our beloved friend, yet we constantly think and speak of him, sharing memorable experiences. He will always be special to us, and we will never forget the love, joy, pride, and humor he gave us. I hope my words have provided the reader with what a unique creature Amos indeed was. I have written these words to honor this incredible athlete, competitor, and FRIEND. Of the hundreds of horses I have dealt with over the years, no other horse ever came close to what he was and always will be in our hearts. He is in heaven, giving God much pride and honor as he watches Amos perform his magic. Shining like a glowing diamond in the sky.

<u>Lovely Amos</u>

Taken June of 1987, Condition and ready for the show ring.

January 1987, One week into his basic groundwork training.